Libra Princesses

Libra Princesses

C. N. Phillips

www.urbanbooks.net

Urban Books, LLC
300 Farmingdale Road, NY-Route 109
Farmingdale, NY 11735

ISBN 13: 978-1-64556-658-8

First Mass Market Printing October 2024
First Trade Paperback Printing October 2023
Printed in the United States of America

10 9 8 7 6 5 4 3 2 1

This is a work of fiction. Any references or similarities to actual events, real people, living or dead, or to real locales are intended to give the novel a sense of reality. Any similarity in other names, characters, places, and incidents is entirely coincidental.

Distributed by Kensington Publishing Corp.
Submit Orders to:
Customer Service
400 Hahn Road
Westminster, MD 21157-4627
Phone: 1-800-733-3000
Fax: 1-800-659-2436

Libra Princesses

From the mind of

C. N. Phillips

This book is dedicated to everyone who is chasing a dream or transforming an old one.

—C. N.

Prologue

"No! I don't want my girls involved in whatever shit you have going on!"

The annoyed woman's shout was followed by the sound of fine china shattering on the wall. Nat Porter, a 40-year-old veteran, had ducked out of the way right on time. It would have been bad business to walk around with a bruised face. A bubble of frustration formed inside him as he stood up straight to face his angry wife.

"Chasity, I wouldn't ask this of them if it weren't important."

"They just started college, Nat. Let them have a life."

"If Zeus doesn't get what he wants—" Nat stopped and sighed as his eyes pled with Chasity. "I just need the journal."

"My grandmother gifted them that journal," Chasity started with a trembling bottom lip. "All of her grandfather, his grandfather, and his grandfather's life's work is in that book. They traveled the world many times to fill it, and you *want them to just hand it over to you so you can do what? Just give it to that drug dealer?"*

There was no reasoning with her, and Nat grew increasingly frustrated. The journal in question wasn't just any journal. It belonged to the world-celebrated archeologist Giovanni. Inside it was a thief or pirate's dream . . . all of his family's rare findings. Findings that were worth a fortune. The existence of Giovanni's journal had been a myth until recently, when Zeus found proof of its existence at an art exhibit. Ever since, he'd been obsessed with finding it. And that alone was enough to put the fear of God into Nat's heart. What Zeus didn't know was that Nat's wife was a direct descendant of Giovanni, and the journal he wanted so badly had been gifted to Nat's daughters. If somehow the trail led Zeus to them, Nat didn't know how he would protect them. Zeus had hundreds of men at his beck and call. He controlled Los Angeles and had many powerful players in his back pocket.

"Zeus is a very dangerous man, Chasity," Nat all but begged. "I have to hide the journal."

"Then why do you work for him, huh? Why do you protect him?"

There was nothing that he could tell his wife that she would believe. Nat didn't think any of his words had even penetrated her skull. Zeus Daniels wasn't just LA's biggest kingpin and most feared man. He was also Nat's cousin. When Nat returned from his last tour, he settled down with his wife and children. Still having a soldier's mentality, he took on a job as security detail for his cousin. Since they'd grown up together, Zeus's lifestyle was nothing new to Nat. Before he left for the army, Nat had seen precisely how Zeus had come up in the game, and it wasn't pretty. He wasn't just brutal. He was merciless. And the new money tree he stumbled upon made him twice that.

Zeus had taken up a fascination with collecting rare items, the kind most would only find in museums. After discovering how much the black market would pay for such items, he became addicted to the trade. Zeus would do whatever it took to find and procure the item he was looking for. He didn't care how much blood was shed in the process.

Nat realized that his own family was in trouble when rumors about Giovanni's journal started floating around. To everyone else, it was nonsense. A man documenting the locations of all those treasures and not taking any for his own gain was unheard of. But to Giovanni's family, it was a rite of passage. When it was Chasity's turn, she had no interest in the world's secrets, and the journal just collected dust. However, it picked right back up with their daughters. Nobody ever

guessed that their family's niche would end up being its curse. Nat knew that his daughters would
die before handing over the journal, and so would
Chasity. That was why Nat was determined to
destroy it before Zeus followed the scent to his
girls.

"Chasity—"

"No, Nat. That book contains my family's legacy."

"You don't understand. Zeus knows that book
exists. Do you know what's in it? Do you know
exactly what your ancestors documented?"

"I do. There are magnificent findings in the
journal from all around the world. Things that
may never be found again."

"Exactly. And that makes them lost treasures.
Treasures that they saw with their own two eyes
and felt with their own hands. Hundreds of them.
That book is a real-life treasure map. If Zeus gets
it, he'll be the richest man in the world."

"So why do you want him to have—"

"I don't want to give it to Zeus. I want to destr—"
Nat was cut off when his phone rang. He saw it
was Zeus after he pulled it out of his pocket and
held a finger up to Chasity. "Hello?"

"I need you to come to Spot One—now," Zeus's
deep voice sounded from the other end.

"Is everything okay?"

"No, it's not. We just got robbed, and I know
who was behind it. I need you to handle it for me."

"No problem. You know I'll get them."

"I hope so."

Nat disconnected the phone and focused his attention back on his wife. The look on her beautiful face was a mixture of disappointment and disgust. And Nat couldn't say that he blamed her. What he was asking of her was a lot on her shoulders. And he couldn't imagine taking something so priceless from his girls, but it had to be done.

"Please just call Nadi and Nori. Have them come home tonight for dinner, okay? I love you."

"I love you too."

He kissed her on the cheek and left the house to handle the job Zeus had for him. Once inside his tan Durango, he checked the magazine in his pistol before tucking it into the holster on his hip. Already strapped to one of his ankles was the .22 revolver he kept there, and strapped to the other ankle was a knife. Many of the things in the army never left him, especially his inability to trust the world around him.

Nat was a specialist in hand-to-hand combat and an expert marksman as well. The training he'd learned in the field, he taught to his children. After working for Zeus, he knew how ugly the streets of LA could get, and he wanted his daughters to be able to protect themselves. He might have gone a little overboard with it because, by the time he was done with their training, they *were miniature soldiers themselves. However, despite what he did in the dark for Zeus, he still wanted them to have normal lives. He didn't want them ever to have to use their training, but it was better to be ready than having to get ready.*

He drove toward the spot Zeus had asked him to meet at. He was slightly shocked by the location Zeus had chosen, mainly because he rarely dropped by there. That particular stash spot was located in South Central. Since Zeus had moved to millionaire status, he barely visited the hood. When Nat inquired why he'd have a part of his location there in the first place, Zeus's answer was simple. "My people blend in here."

When Nat arrived, he noticed two black SUVs outside the property. He parked and walked to the duplex on the right. As soon as he approached, the door opened, and he was ushered inside by another one of Zeus's hired hands, Trey. He was young, about the same age as Nat's girls, but one thing was different for sure . . . He was deadly. However, Nat had gotten to know him and had taken quite a liking to the kid. Trey had a good heart. He was just doing what he had to do to care for his family.

"What's up, Nat? Zeus is in the back," Trey said, nodding his head for Nat to follow him. "You good?"

"Yup. Just here to handle what needs to be handled," Nat said as they walked. "He tell you what's going on?"

"Nah. He called me here and told me some shit needs to be handled. Probably some crazy motherfucka moving in on the turf again. You remember what happened to the last folks that did that?"

"Yeah." Nat smirked. "I was the one who did it to them."

"You're a cold piece, Nat. You gotta teach me some of that army shit one day."

Nat didn't get a chance to answer because they had reached the back room by then. Standing around a red chair were three more of Zeus's people, and sitting in the chair was Zeus himself. He was wearing an expensive suit and puffing a Cuban cigar like he had no care in the world. When he saw the newcomers enter, he put the cigar out and got up from his chair.

"It's about time you showed up," he bellowed and hugged Nat.

"My bad, cuz. I had to wrap up some stuff at home," Nat said when they released each other.

"Wifey tripping?"

"Something like that," Nat said, not breaking eye contact. "What's up, though? You said somebody robbed you?"

Before Zeus answered, he walked to a table on one side of the room and poured himself a glass of brandy. He gestured to Nat to see if he wanted some, but Nat declined. Whatever the job was, Nat wanted to get it done so he could go home. He waited for Zeus to down the entire glass and return to his seat.

"The sundial bracelet that I recently acquired is missing. Along with the ancient robes worn by King Tut himself." Zeus shook his head. "Gone. Do you know how long it took me to find those items? How much they're worth? I have a buyer ready this instant to take them off my hands, but it seems that somebody already did that."

"Do you know who's responsible?" Nat asked in an even tone.

Zeus stared at him for a while, not blinking. Nat's facial expression stayed the same, and he didn't move. Finally, a smirk came to Zeus's face.

"Yes, I do. Actually, I have the culprit here now." Zeus motioned his head at one of the goons, and the big man disappeared briefly. When he returned, he dragged a woman with disheveled hair and bloody clothes. "That's her right there."

Her eyes were swollen shut, indicating that she'd been beaten badly. Her breathing was labored, and even if she weren't bound and gagged, it was doubtful she'd be able to move very much. It wasn't just her blood-soaked clothes that made

Nate swallow a lump in his throat. It was the fact that he knew her.

"Lilah," he breathed sadly, seeing his partner in such bad shape.

Both he and Lilah shared the same passion, and that was not wanting to see someone like Zeus obtain more power than he already had. Zeus wasn't just on the prowl for valuable relics. He wanted the priceless ones. The ones collectors on the black market would sell their souls for. Through his children, Nat had a newfound respect for the artifacts Zeus collected. They weren't just treasures with a price tag on them. They were pieces of history. Lilah shared the same sentiment. It wasn't hard for her to get into Zeus's bed, nor was it hard for them to smuggle many of Zeus's findings out of his clutches and to their rightful cultures.

"I-I'm sorry," Lilah said weakly. "I didn't have a choice."

Nat didn't need to ask her what she meant. He had his answer when he looked back into his cousin's eyes. Zeus knew everything. Before Nat could move, Zeus snapped his fingers and put his men on him. Nat tried to reach his gun, but one of Zeus's men grabbed his arm and pinned it behind his back. Another punched him hard in the face, disorienting him for a few moments. The men disarmed him of everything in those moments while Trey stood on the side, looking confused.

"What . . . What's going on?" Trey asked.

"You're about to see what happens to traitors. Blood means nothing if it's disloyal," Zeus said while Nat was forced to his knees. Zeus drew his gun and screwed a silencer on before looking at Lilah. "I guess now isn't the best time to tell you that you were great in bed. What a waste."

He aimed the weapon at her forehead, and Nat fought against the men restraining him. She was a good woman. She didn't deserve to die like that. But it was no use. Zeus pulled the trigger once, and the bullet hit her square in the forehead. Nat witnessed her last breath, and his heart sank into his stomach. It was then that he realized he'd never see his family again.

"Why would you do it?" Zeus asked, turning to him. "You cost me millions. Millions."

"I did what I had to do," Nat said. "We stole them because those artifacts belong to their cultures, not in the sitting room of a rich schmuck like you."

Zeus's nose flared at the silence that followed. Maybe he thought his cousin would beg for his life, but there he knelt, defiant as ever. Maybe he wanted Nat to give him a reason to keep him alive, but he didn't. The silence was what made Zeus angry. He was used to men groveling, but Nat was firm in his decision.

Zeus clenched his jaw and aimed the gun at Nat's chest, but he stopped himself from pulling the trigger at the last second. His men paid attention to the hesitation, perhaps thinking he would be lenient because the two men were family. But really, their being family didn't do anything but make Zeus want to make an example of Nat even more. Finally, he tucked the gun away, and Nat emptied the breath in his chest but sucked it right back in when he saw the knife Zeus pulled from his jacket. With it clenched in his hand and a quick thrust, Zeus grunted and plunged the blade through Nat's heart. Zeus placed a hand on his shoulder and bent slightly to speak in his ear.

"Just doing what I have to do," he said, listening to Nat take his last breath.

When he removed the knife from his chest, Zeus felt the remainder of Nat's life come with it. The men holding Nat let him fall to the floor as blood spilled from his wound. Zeus turned to a horrified Trey and wiped the knife off on the young man's arm. Nobody knew what to say, so Zeus gave one final instruction.

"Clean this up."

Chapter 1

Nori

Three years later

The moment I heard the crashing sound of glass shattering, my hands flew to the top of my freshly installed sew-in. I wasn't the one who had dropped the tray of drinks, but I might as well have been. I took a deep breath to keep the intense feeling of annoyance at bay, but a groan slipped through my lips anyway. When anything happened in the restaurant I worked at, somehow, the blame always came back to me, especially if the person that messed up was my boss's niece, Trish.

I worked at a restaurant called Sebastian's, a place for fine dining. People from all over Los Angeles came there to eat. They even had a photo wall dedicated to all the celebrities who had dined there. I was behind the bar, and Trish had just left after grabbing the final drink for her table before she tripped over her own feet. She went crashing down, along with the tray in her hands.

"Dammit, Trish," I groaned.

"I know, I know," she said, looking at the damage she'd done.

She looked like she wanted to cry, and I wanted like hell to be mad at her. I couldn't, though. I knew that day her mind was all over the place since it was close to her parents' death anniversary. They had died in a car accident when she was just a teenager, and she'd been living with Tera, her aunt, ever since. Not only that, but Trish was also just like me. We were both in our early twenties, working a dead-end job just to get by, so some days wouldn't be as good as others. The only thing was, she always got off easy. Me, on the other hand? Tera couldn't stand me.

I held out my hand and helped Trish to her feet. We both checked her to make sure she didn't have any cuts. By then, the bus boys had already made their way over to clean up the mess. It was a good thing it was a slow Tuesday night, and all the guests were seated at the far side of the restaurant. Still, it was only a matter of time before—

"Norielle, what did you do?" I heard Tera's angry voice before I saw her.

Sighing, I slowly turned around to face the raging bull. Tera was a caramel-complexioned

Black woman like Trish. She was a big-boned woman in her fifties and always wore a ponytail in her graying hair. Her brown eyes glared down her pointy nose at me like she wanted to snatch me up.

"Aunt Tera, it wasn't Nori. It was me. I dropped the tray," Trish hurried to say, but Tera held up her hand to silence her.

"Did you or did you not just come from the bar?" Tera asked her but kept her eyes on me.

"I did, but—"

"Norielle, how often must I tell you to ensure the tray is well-balanced before letting someone walk off with it?"

Her reasons for blaming me for everything got more outlandish by the day, and I wasn't even surprised. I didn't know what it was about me that she couldn't stand, but I didn't care. She could shove that dislike where the sun didn't shine.

"I *did* make sure the tray was balanced before I let her take it," I said, trying to keep my voice calm. "The tray wasn't the problem. She tripped. What are you going to do, blame me for not tying her shoes? Now, excuse me. I need to remake those drinks."

Tera's face turned red, and I could tell she wanted to curse me out, but she knew I was right. I remade the drinks for Trish and almost decided to take the drinks over to the guests myself. What stopped me was remembering that I was nobody's slave. Trish was a sweet girl, but she had her job that night, and I had mine. I handed the tray to her, making sure that it was balanced well before turning to roll my eyes at Tera.

Yes, she was my boss, but a person could only take so much. I fought with myself not to quit every day. The availability was flexible with my school schedule, and the customers always left handsome tips. Tera just seemed to like to press my buttons. If I didn't know any better, I'd think she was trying to get rid of me.

"Is it proper etiquette to roll your eyes at your boss?" she asked, leaning her big bosoms on the bar. "I could fire you right now if I wanted to."

"But you won't because then, you'd have to deal with Ed, you know, the *real* boss and person who owns this place," I shot back at her.

"Trust me. Ed won't do anything to me if I let you go."

"I'm sure he will once I hit him with a lawsuit listing all the ways you harass me. And those will back up all my claims," I said, pointing at one of the cameras facing the bar.

Tera looked up, and her face grew red again. Seeing that I had her in a bind, I felt a small jolt of pleasure. However, she would have to wait if she wanted to say anything else to me. A group of guys entered the restaurant and sat at the bar. Turning my back on the angry bull, I sashayed over to the men, showing off my pearly whites.

"Good afternoon, gentlemen. What can I get started for you guys?"

After a long day of working and flirting for my tips, I made it home with an extra $500 in my pocket. I all but dragged my feet to my bedroom in my condo. Tossing the money on the mahogany dresser underneath my mounted television, I stripped out of my black work uniform. It was almost eleven o'clock, and all I wanted to do was take a hot shower and hop in bed. But Netflix was calling my name, and I had a date with Sam and Dean Winchester.

I went to my en suite bathroom and put a shower cap over my fresh do. I would be damned if I paid $400 for my hair to get wet and sweat out. My bathroom was probably my favorite part of the condo. It was huge, and I loved the enclosed shower. But there was also a deep tub positioned right by the window that gave the most beautiful view of the city. And built into the long sink counter was a vanity that held all my beauty secrets. My bathroom was a safe place to release and transform. I wished I had the energy to take a long bath and gaze at the lively city below, but I was drained. Turning the knob for the shower, I got in and let the water have its way with me.

After the water cleansed my body of the day, I got out and wrapped a towel around me. I was about to do my nightly facial routine when I heard something fall to the floor. It had come from the front of the condo. Instead of grabbing my facial moisturizer, I opened one of the drawers of my vanity and grabbed my .22. As quietly as I could, I crept out of my bedroom and down the hallway. The gun was aimed, and my back slid against the wall. I could hear someone moving around, and I could also see their shadow in the moonlight.

"You broke into the wrong spot, motherfucka," I shouted, flicking on the light.

My finger was on the trigger, but I stopped myself from pulling it at the last minute when I saw who was bustling around my kitchen. Dressed in black cargo jeans and a hoodie was none other than my sister, Nadi. In her hands were a sandwich and a gallon of lemonade.

"Damn, sis, were you about to shoot me?" she asked, amused, and took a big bite of the sandwich.

"Nadi, what are you doing here?" I asked, lowering the gun and placing it on the island bar in the kitchen.

"Last I checked, my name is the one on the lease, and my bedroom is down the hall," she said in her usual smart-mouthed nature. She sat down at the dining room table and looked at the towel I was wearing. "Where are your clothes?"

"I just got out of the shower. Why don't you call before you just show up? And—" I rushed and snatched the lemonade from her hand when she went to drink from the jug. "Get a glass."

"Unclench your ass cheeks. Damn," she said, rolling her eyes and taking another bite of her sandwich. "And since when do I have to call before I show up?"

"Since you almost got shot. You haven't been here in weeks, and you haven't returned any of my calls or texts."

"I've been working."

"Yeah, working," I scoffed.

"Not tonight, Norielle," she groaned. "I don't want to hear one of your lectures right now."

"I'm just saying, you can check in every once in a while."

"What do you think I'm doing now?" she said with a smirk and finished her food.

"Uugh," I shouted and threw up my hands. "One day, you're going to get hurt really bad, and I'm not even going to have a clue where you are." I couldn't even look at her. I turned away and went back to my bedroom to get dressed. As I put on my pajamas, I found myself sighing. Nadi and I were two weeks apart. Back in the day, our father, an ex-marine, had gotten quite busy. His name was Nat Porter, and he was a handsome man who moved from state to state. He was a hit with the women wherever he went, so much so that he got two women pregnant at the same time.

Chasity, Nadi's mom, and our dad were married shortly after Nadi was born. I was sure she thought she would live happily ever after with her husband and new baby in their big house. They did . . . for a while. However, on one fateful day, their lives changed forever, and so did mine.

"Mama, where are we going?" 10-year-old me asked from the backseat of my mama's Buick.

I stared at the back of my mother's red wig, waiting for her answer. But she didn't. She just continued driving fast. I looked out the window at the unfamiliar neighborhood. The houses were so big, like the ones I saw on my favorite TV shows. Like the ones I hoped I could live in one day. With Mama working all those hours at the club at night, maybe it would happen soon.

I looked back up at the front seat at my mama, that time staring at her through the rearview mirror. She looked . . . angry. Well, she was always mad at something. Most times, it was me. I couldn't seem to do anything right in her eyes. But I didn't know why she looked so mad that time, and she hadn't said much to me that day. The only time she talked to me was when she told me to get dressed so we could go.

"Mama—"

"We're here," she cut me off.

Our blue Buick turned into the long driveway. I felt my eyes grow big when I looked up at the house it was connected to. It reminded me of a smaller version of the house in Home Alone. *I felt myself growing excited and hoping I could go in.*

"Mama, who lives here?" I asked.

"Come on," she said, ignoring me again.

She opened her door and got out in a hurry. I was still too busy staring at the house to notice her grab a suitcase from the trunk. But when I saw it, my excitement turned to curiosity. Slowly, I got out of the car and shut the door behind me. She grabbed my arm and pulled me alongside her as we walked fast to the door. Before ringing the doorbell, she fixed her wig and checked her reflection in the window.

Ding dong. Ding dong.

She rang twice, and I could hear it from where we stood. Moments later, I heard someone come to the door, but it didn't open. They were probably looking at us through the peephole. Finally, the door unlocked and swung open. On the other side, looking down at me, was a tall, dark man. He had waves in his short haircut and a beard. Something was familiar about his brown eyes, sharp jaw, and the shape of his full lips. I stared back at him until Mama cleared her throat.

"Long time no see, Nat," she said, and when he looked at her, he seemed genuinely shocked to see her.

"T-Tammy? What are you doing here?" he asked, then glanced over his shoulder.

"I'm here because I'm tired." Mama put her free hand on her hip.

"Tired of what, Tammy?"

"Tired of taking care of your daughter all by myself. That's what."

"Daughter?" Nat asked, bewildered. "My daughter is upstairs playing with her dolls."

"Well, tell her she has a sister that wants to play too."

I couldn't believe what I was hearing. He was my . . . dad? I didn't know I had one of those. Well, of course, I did, but Mama didn't talk about him much. I thought maybe he was dead or something. The more I stared at him, the more it made sense why his features were so familiar. They were the same ones I saw in the mirror every day.

"Tammy, don't be showing up at my door starting no mess now. I've moved on and started a family."

"Don't flatter yourself. You weren't anything but a good lay. One that gave me a child. You don't remember?" Mama rolled her neck.

"You said you lost that baby."

"Well, I lied. I just was tired of your two-timing ass," Mama told him.

"What the hell is wrong with you? And then just to show up at my door?"

"I tried to contact you after I had her, but by then, you'd moved home to Virginia. So when I found out you'd moved back here, I thought I'd bring you a present. Does your wife know how loose with that meat package you were?"

"She . . . can't be mine, can she?" he asked, looking back at me. "How old are you, sweetheart?"

"Ten last month."

"Last month?" he asked, wide-eyed.

"Why are you looking so shocked? We fooled around ten years ago."

"It's not that. It's just that I—"

"Daddy?" a small voice sounded.

A little girl around my age appeared on the side of him. She looked . . . like me, except she had lighter skin and eyes. She shifted her focus from her dad to us and then back to him.

"Nadia, go back upstairs with Mommy. Daddy will be inside soon."

"Who's she?" Nadia asked, pointing at me.

"This is your sister," Mama said and glared at Nat. "I'm not taking care of your responsibility anymore. I don't want this, and I don't want her."

"Nat, honey, what's going on?" another voice sounded.

A beautiful woman with the same light complexion as Nadia came to the door. She stood next to her husband with a confused look on her face. Her eyes fell on Mama and then on me. When she saw me, she gave a small gasp.

"Chasity, baby, take Nadia back upstairs."

"After you tell me who these people are."

"Tell her," Mama said with a smirk.

There was an awkward silence. The excitement that I'd felt before had worn off completely. All I wanted to do was run back to the car, but I didn't think Mama would let me. The suitcase made sense to me finally. She was trying to leave me.

"This is . . . This is Tammy."

"Tammy? The only Tammy I know is the one you used to mess with back in the day before we got together."

"That would be the one," Nat said awkwardly and cleared his throat, looking back and forth between the two women. After a moment of the two of them glaring at each other, Nat motioned to me. "This is her daughter. I . . . she . . . She says this is my daughter too. And I think she is."

Chasity's mouth fell open, and hurt spread across her face. Her eyes fell on me, and for some reason, I felt shame. It was an emotion that brought tears to my eyes. I felt unwanted, and I wished I could hide. She saw my tears, and instantly, the hurt expression on her face turned to concern. She stepped forward and knelt so she was at eye level with me.

"What's your name?"

"Norielle. But everyone calls me Nori."

"Nori. I like that. How old are you, baby girl?"

"Ten last month."

"Ten . . . last month? In October?"

"Yes. On the fifth."

"Wow," Chasity said and looked up at Nat. "Two weeks apart. Really?"

"I'm sorry, baby. Before I met you, I was a little loose," Nat said sheepishly. "I didn't know I had another kid."

Chasity's eyes went to the suitcase, and she stood up. Mama had a smug look on her face, while Chasity had disgust on hers. The two women had a stare down before one of them spoke.

"So, you're just going to drop her off on the steps to strangers?" Chasity asked in disbelief.

"He ain't no stranger. He's her daddy."

"No, he's a man she doesn't know."

"Either way, she ain't coming home with me. I'm sick of her. I never wanted to be a mom. I have dreams, and she's just holding me back. Every time I wake up and see her, she makes me sick." Mama looked at me and turned up her nose. "If y'all don't want her, I'll take her and drop her off somewhere."

Her words hurt worse than any whooping she'd ever given me. The tears ran down my face in two streams. Nadia rushed by her parents and threw her arms around me. Her hug was tight and comforting. So naturally, I hugged her back. When she pulled away from me, she wiped my tears and glared at Mama. The words that came out of her mouth next were so strong and heartfelt for her to be only 10 like me.

"My sister is home," she said, looking at her parents. "Mommy? Daddy?"

"There's no question what has to be done," Chasity said, and I just knew she was going to tell Nadia that I couldn't stay. But then she smiled at me.

"Come inside, baby," Nat said and held his hand out to me. "We'll figure out all of this."

I came back to the present and wiped away the single tear that had fallen from my eye. Thinking back to that day always made me emotional. My birth mother really dropped me off and went on about her life. That was the last time I'd ever seen her. Thank God she'd been right about Nat being my father, which a DNA test later proved. Learning about my dad's past wasn't easy on Chasity, but from that very first day on, she loved and treated me like her daughter. And Nadi? Nadi had always been my sister since the first time we laid eyes on each other.

"I know you didn't come in here so you could cry."

I turned my head to see my sister leaning on the doorway. I expected her to be smirking, but she looked genuinely concerned. Still, I rolled my eyes.

"Nobody is in here crying over you," I told her. I was about to turn away but saw something sticking out of her hoodie pocket. It was a black ski mask. "You're going on a job tonight, aren't you?"

"Tap your nose. That's none of your business."

"It *is* my business. You're my sister. You have to stop this shit. Kelz is a bad influence on you, Nadi."

"Watch your mouth. You don't know shit about Kelz."

"I know he's the reason why you dropped out of school. I also know he's using you for your knowledge and for all the shit Daddy taught us. Dirty money isn't good money, Nadia."

"You don't say that when you take my dirty money to pay for this condo. Or to pay for that Benz you ride in and tuition whenever the money from that little restaurant job falls short. You could never have none of this if it weren't for me."

"When Daddy died, we told each other we would forget our training and become archeologists. He thought the world was so ugly that we needed to be prepared for anything. Do you remember how much we hated going to training? We were kids learning how to kill people. We promised each other that since we couldn't control how ugly the world could be, we would discover its beauty."

"That's what I'm doing. So while you're in school trying to get your degree, I'm actually in the field doing what we promised."

"It's not the same. You steal artifacts for a living and sell them on the black market, Nadi," I shouted.

"And doing so has made me a rich woman, Nori. It's made *us* rich. I drive a fucking McLaren, and I've been all around the world."

"You should preserve the things you find, not sell them."

"Preserve them for what? So some damn museum can showcase them? You *do* realize that they do the exact same thing that I do, just with a pretty bow wrapped."

"You didn't get like this until you met Kelz," I said, shaking my head. "He uses you. Why can't you see it?"

I could tell that my words bothered her by the angry flare that crossed over her eyes. Her boyfriend was always a touchy subject. Especially because I was never secretive about my dislike for him. Before he met my sister, he was known in LA as a big-time thief and scammer. However, when he met Nadi, the score got bigger. She knew about many lost artifacts worldwide and had connections on how to find them. The Nadi I used to know would have been okay with just holding her findings in her hands one time. But Kelz turned her into a miniature version of himself—a thief.

"We use each other. That's how love works," she snarled at me.

"Love? You think he loves you? You're the biggest meal ticket he's ever had. Without you, none of it works. That's *not* love, Nadi."

"You know what?" she scoffed. "I came here to check on my sister, but I see now that all you want to do is judge me. You want to talk about promises we made before life really kicked in? Fine, I'll let you have that by yourself. I don't want to struggle like you, and if I don't do this, we won't eat. So *you* can let your knowledge and training go to waste. But me? I'ma make some bread."

She turned and stormed out of the room. I wanted to let her leave, but I couldn't. My thoughts went back to the first hug she'd given me. And she was right. She was always there for me when I needed it. But that didn't mean I agreed with her lifestyle. However, no matter what, she was still my blood. I chased her and caught her right as she opened the door.

"Nadi," I said, grabbing her arm.

"What?" she said, annoyed, and snatched away.

"What I said . . . I get it. I really do. I just worry about you."

"You don't need to worry about me."

"But I do. I love you more than anything in this world. You're my sister. Just—" I paused briefly and looked into her eyes. "Just check in sometimes. Okay? And whatever you're doing tonight, please, be careful."

The hardness on her face softened, and she nodded.

"Okay," she said and was gone.

Chapter 2

Nadi

I didn't want to admit it, but my sister's words had really gotten under my skin. Especially when she mentioned our father. It could have been because she had the nerve to say it to my face or because I knew my dad wouldn't be happy with me. If he knew what I was doing with the training he'd given us, he would probably roll over in his grave. As an ex-marine, he prepared Nori and me for a world most people ignored. He knew that anything could happen at any given time and wanted us ready for it.

At the ripe old age of 11 was when Nori and I began our combat training. And by 13, we could take a full-grown man down. Then at 14, our dad taught us to shoot every caliber gun. He took us to the range daily, and we worked on our aim. On still targets at first, and once we got our aim right, we graduated to moving targets. He was a master marksman and didn't rest until we were better than him.

I drove my baby-blue McLaren as if I had stolen it, and before I knew it, I'd arrived at the hideout. It was an apartment complex in downtown LA that Kelz rented under an alias. Our crew would meet there before a job, and that night was no different. After I parked, I went inside and took the elevator up to the top. When I got off, I pushed Nori's words to the back of my mind. I didn't need anything throwing me off. Finally, I reached the apartment door and did the secret knock.

Knock, knock. Pause. *Knock, knock, knock.*

I stepped away from the black door and waited for someone to open it. When they did, a big smile came over my face. Seeing Kelz instantly put me in a good mood with his fine self. The first thing I noticed was the fresh braids on his head. The next was the crisp lineup and taper he had around them. Kelz was a tall man. He towered above my five-foot-seven frame like a giant. His muscular frame told that he worked out a lot. In our line of work, being fit was a must.

He licked his full lips and looked down at me with his mahogany eyes. The next thing I knew, I was in his arms, accepting a deep, wet kiss from him.

"What took you so long?" he asked in his deep country voice when our lips parted.

"I stopped by to see my sister," I said.

"She still hate me?"

"You know it," I said, grinning.

He let me go, and I stepped inside the apartment. I expected to see three additional people, but only one person was sitting on the sectional in the living room. It was Banks. He and Kelz had traveled to LA from Houston years ago. It was fresh territory, and nobody knew their faces, which made it easier for them to move around. They'd made a business out of being thieves. Before Kelz met me, they'd hit almost every notorious name in LA, from rappers, to drug lords, and even athletes. And to that day, nobody knew what they looked like. They were true professionals.

"Where's Charles and Coney?" I asked, looking around for the other two members of the crew.

They'd come from Houston too, but it was apparent that Banks and Kelz ran the show.

"They aren't makin' it on this go-round," Banks said, focusing on something on his phone screen.

"What do you mean they aren't going to make it?" I asked, feeling a slight sense of alarm coming over me. I turned to Kelz to fact-check. "What's he talking about?"

"They're preoccupied with something else right now, but the three of us can handle this job," Kelz told me, taking a seat on the sectional.

I let out a big breath and briefly put my hands on my face. It had taken weeks of preparation to get ready for this job, and it was already going to crap before we left. There was no way the three of us could pull it off, not alone.

"Please, tell me you're joking," I said when I removed my hands.

"Baby, we can do this."

"Do you know how valuable this artifact is? It's only surfaced twice in a century, and this is the second time. If we fuck this up, we won't have another chance to get it. *And* we'll be out of a million dollars, not to mention Daugherty will never work with us again."

To calm myself down, I started pacing back and forth. The thing we were after was a sword, but not just any sword. It was forged of pure gold, and the hilt was made entirely from diamonds. It dated back to ancient Rome and was said to be so heavy that only a god could wield it. It was one of three lost treasures of King Romulus. We'd found two so far for our buyer, and this sword was the last one. It took a while, but I'd finally been able to trace it to a professor named John Berkley.

Ironically, Professor Berkley had taught my archeology class before I dropped out. He also worked at a local museum, procuring rare items for it. One might understand my excitement when I learned that he finally got his hands on the sword named after Death himself. News in my circle traveled fast, especially regarding things coming and going from every museum in California. I might not have finished school to get my degree, but my connections were as solid as they came. One of them was millionaire Christopher Daugherty. He was a man who loved collecting rare artifacts and knew what kind of business I was in. He'd already given us $500,000 each for the crown of Romulus and his armor. I wasn't willing to drop the ball on the sword.

"No," I said, shaking my head at Kelz and Banks. "I've been the only one sticking my neck out for almost two years. Now isn't the time to go in half-assed."

"The only one stickin' your neck out?" Banks looked up at me from his phone with his nose turned up. "The last time I checked, we all were divin' in headfirst for these jobs."

"But if it weren't for me, we would have no one to hire us."

"Don't act like we weren't in the game before you hopped in," he said.

"Yeah, robbing safes with maybe a hundred thousand. Split between y'all, that's only twenty-five thousand. You weren't catching big fish until I came around. This is a whole new ball game for y'all, and you know it just like I do," I told him and then turned to Kelz. "Getting this job done for

Daugherty is important. We need his connections. What was the point of casing Professor Berkley's house for the past week? You need to call those motherfuckas so they can get here *now*. We have work to do."

Kelz and Banks looked at each other. Banks sighed big and shrugged his shoulders before returning to his phone. Kelz stood up and approached me, taking my hands in his.

"Something came up. They're not going to be able to come tonight, Nadi. So the three of us are what we have. We'll have to make it work."

"Do you know exactly what it is we're after?" I asked. "This is Thanatos we're talking about, the sword of death."

"I know what's on the line."

"Then what about the plan?"

"The plan is going to stay the same. It's gonna work. We don't have anything to worry about. Do you trust me, Nadi?" He pulled me to him and stared deeply into my soul. I hated when he did that because if it were my soul he asked for, I would give it to him while I was in that trance. "Nadi?"

"Fine," I said. "But this shit better not get us killed. So let's load up."

I left them in the front room and headed to the master bedroom. Once there, I closed the door behind me to have some privacy. Then slowly walking to the bed, I knelt on the floor and pulled out a long safe from underneath. After inputting the code, I slid it open and stared at a pistol. Its slide was chrome, and beside it were two fully loaded magazines.

As I stared at it, I felt my heartbeat quicken. I thought the nerves and butterflies I felt before a job would disappear after my first time in the field. But there I was, many jobs later, still having the same feelings. I used to think it was adrenaline, but I knew now that it was fear . . . of getting caught or something worse than that. What I did was very dangerous, but in a world of light and dark, it was a fact that the underworld paid the bills. I took a deep breath and snatched the gun and ammo. It was time to go.

Chapter 3

Zeus

"Ooh, shit. Just like that," I encouraged the curly-haired, beautiful Brazilian woman on her knees before me.

The tip of my manhood was at the furthest point in her mouth, and she tried her best not to choke. Spit ran down her chin and onto her bare, perky breasts. Her name was Shalia, and although she wasn't much good for anything else around my mansion, she knew how to please me. I wanted to enjoy the fellatio for a while longer, but when I glanced at the clock in my master bedroom, I knew I would have to speed it up. I was expecting company.

I gripped the sides of Shalia's head with my hands and thrust in and out of her mouth. She tried her best to keep up with me and with the feeling of her tongue sliding against my shaft and the warmth of her mouth, my climax was forced out of me. I shot my soldiers down her esophagus and threw my head back ecstatically.

"Whew. Hell yeah. *That's* what the fuck I'm talking about," I all but shouted.

Once she finished swallowing, she stood up, showcasing her thick, naked body. There wasn't a blemish in sight. Shalia was 25 years old and was the latest addition to my house. Three other women lived with me and took care of all my needs. Naturally, a man of my stature couldn't have just one woman. Things got messy that way. I preferred a woman who knew her place and didn't take one step out of it. She grinned at me as I breathed deeply, knowing she had done her job well.

"Is there anything else you need, Zeus?" she asked.

"Yes. Have Kiara ready some refreshments. We're about to have guests. Nothing too fancy, though."

She nodded but didn't leave. Instead, she just stared at me like something was on the tip of her tongue. She was still new and learning how things operated around there. But soon, she would realize that once my use of her was over, she needed to be gone out of my sight.

"What?"

"It's just . . . You got Kiara a new Chanel bag, and Pamela just went on a shopping spree. I was wondering—"

"You were wondering if you could get a bag or shopping spree?" I asked, and she smiled while nodding her head. "So, I take it that you already spent your allowance?"

"Yes. I had to take care of my mother and siblings back home. *Please*, baby. I'll manage my money better next month, I promise."

There was a reason why they said a woman would always be a man's downfall, especially when he was thinking with his dick. If I wasn't still tingling from the head she'd just given me, and if her body weren't tempting me, I would have told her to get the hell out of my face. I gave all four of my girls a hefty monthly allowance so that I could handle my business without them constantly begging me for something. The rule was when the money was gone, it was gone until the next month. Of course, depending on how happy they made me, I would gift them with things here and there on top of their allowance. I had to admit that Shalia had made me a happy man at that moment, and all I could do was shake my head.

"I'll put something in your account," I said after a few seconds.

She squealed joyfully and wrapped her arms around me, pressing her breasts to my chest. When she pulled back, she kissed me before hurrying out of the room. I was left alone and naked in my bedroom, so I went into the master bathroom to shower. When I finished, I temporarily put on my Versace robe and went to the Men's Wearhouse, I mean, my closet. The space alone was enough to make a person mistake it for a designer store, that and all the expensive clothes inside of it. I bought my first pair of Gucci loafers when I made my first thousand. When I made my first five, I bought a suit to match it. I still had both of those items, although it would take a while to find them in everything I'd accumulated since. I advocated that to be a boss, one must first look like it. Nothing but the finest touched my skin. I was no longer in the mud. I lived in the sky.

I walked over to my black suit section. After I selected one and a pair of loafers to match, I grabbed my favorite diamond cuff links. Not only did I like looking like money, but I also enjoyed smelling like it too. As soon as I was fully dressed, I sprayed Tom Ford Bois Marocain, a scent that could hardly keep my ladies off me.

Leaving my room, I went to my office on the first level of my home. It was in part of the house, away from everything. When it came to business, I liked to be as private as possible, even in my own home. When I got there, I saw my chocolate goddess, Kiara, setting down a tray of finger foods on a glass table at the side of the room. She was a petite woman with a plump rump. Her entire body was covered in tattoos. Most of them were hidden under her jeans and top, but I didn't need a visual to know what was where. I'd tasted every one of them. That evening, she wore her red locs neatly tucked in a bun on top of her head.

Upon seeing me, a broad smile came to her full lips, and she hurried to pull out my desk chair so I could sit down. When I did, she placed a porcelain ashtray in front of me and lit a Cuban cigar.

"There you go, handsome," she said, handing it to me.

"You're too good to me, baby." I took a drag and held the smoke in my chest for a few seconds before blowing it out.

"The best, and don't you forget it."

"How can I with an ass like that?" I asked and took a handful of one of her cheeks in my free hand.

"Mmm, I would have thought you had enough ass for the day," she commented through pursed lips.

I heard a tinge of jealousy in her voice. I wasn't surprised. Out of all my girls, Kiara was the most territorial when it came to me. She had also been the first lady of the house. The two of us went back longer than the others. I'd met her passed out in one of my dope houses and thought she was too beautiful to go out that way. So I put her in rehab, got her clean of the street drugs, and gave her a new one—me. All addiction came at a price, and hers was jealousy. If she had it her way, all my free time would be hers instead of being split between all of them. But it wasn't her way. It was mine.

"Don't start today, Kiara," I warned.

"But—"

"What did I just say?" There was a chill in my tone that made her do away with whatever it was she was about to spill out. I felt her body stiffen in my hand and knew that she wasn't happy. I released her bottom and opted for her hand, kissing it. "Thank you, baby, for the food. You always do what I ask of you. You know I appreciate you, right?"

"Yes."

"Good. What are the other girls doing?"

"Pamela's cleanin' the kitchen, Raven is in her room, and the new girl . . . Well, you know what the new girl was just doing."

The doorbell sounded before I could say anything, and I knew it was who I was expecting. The security I had surrounding my home wouldn't have let anyone else make it to the front door. Kiara left to answer it. A few minutes later, she returned with two men in tow. I motioned toward the table of refreshments for the men to indulge in, which they did, with no questions. Once they filled their plates, they sat in the chairs across from my desk. I turned back to Kiara, who was waiting for me to give her leave.

"Go wait for me in my room. I'll be right up when I finish here. You deserve some one-on-one time."

Her face brightened, and she quickly left the office, shutting the door behind her. I cleared my voice and faced the newcomers. Charles and Coney were their names, and they were cousins, or so they said. I couldn't quite see a resemblance. Charles was tall and had high-yellow skin. The coarse hair on the top of his head was cut short, and he had scars all over his face. I never cared to ask where he'd gotten them. Coney couldn't be more than five foot eight and black as night. His hair was braided straight back in many corn rows. I wasn't gay in the least to judge another man's looks, but the boy was ugly as hell. It was a wonder how he ever got laid. I allowed them to stuff their faces for a few moments. For men who saw a nice chunk of money on a regular, they ate like they hadn't done so for days. Maybe they hadn't, as busy as I was keeping them.

"News?" I finally asked, growing tired of their smacking.

Coney wiped his mouth with a napkin before looking up at me.

"That thing you wanted handled is going down tonight," he told me.

"And you're sure it's authentic?"

"The gir—" Charles started, but Coney interrupted him.

"We know our stuff; trust us," he said quickly and shot Charles a look.

"Oh, I do . . . because we all know what will happen if you fuck up even in the slightest bit," I said, allowing my menacing energy to fill the air. I watched uncomfortable looks come over their faces. "When can I expect it delivered to me?"

"Within a week," Charles answered.

"I'll hold you to it."

"And how much are we getting paid for this little trade-off?" Coney asked.

His face was eager, and I could tell he expected me to answer. However, I only discussed what was absolutely necessary with the help.

"You can take up your cut with your boss. Kelz will make sure you get your money."

"Boss?" Coney asked.

"The one who calls the shots and tells you about the jobs, right? Seems to me that if it weren't for him, you both would be out of work. Sounds like a boss to me."

"Right," Coney said without challenging my words. "Kelz said he'll contact you about the meeting spot soon. Cool?"

"I'll be expecting the call."

I nodded at the two of them, and they got up and excused themselves. Then I leaned back and turned on the computer on my desk when they left my office. Toggling to the surveillance screen, I tapped my fingers together as I watched the men walk to the front door. Coney seemed to have a bad case of short man's syndrome. He always had an angry undertone. I could sense his agitation through the screen as it looked like he and Charles were in some sort of spat. Whatever it was about, Coney was visibly upset.

As long as it didn't get in the way of our business, I didn't care. Whatever the issue, I was sure they would bring it up with their boss. A lot of money was on the line, and I could already feel my hand itching. Whoever said a man could have too much money or riches was a liar. The artifacts I was finding and selling were small fish compared to the big one I was after. But the small finds would have to do until I finally got my hands on Giovanni's journal.

Chapter 4

Nadi

Underneath the surface, I was still fuming about having to do the job with only three able bodies, but what choice did we have? I wasn't going to let the opportunity pass me by. Plus, by the time we got to the professor's manor, I was just ready to get in and out.

We parked the unmarked vehicle we were in down the street to seem as inconspicuous as possible. Kelz had made the right call by stealing us a black Mercedes. We blended right in.

"Whew," Banks whistled as he leaned to the front of the car. He was eyeing the professor's home, practically drooling. "What kind of college professor do you know that can afford a place like that?"

"The kind that dabbles in a little something something, if you ask me," Kelz noted.

"Or it's owned by the college," I said.

I pulled out a rolled-up piece of parchment from the backpack I'd brought along. I unrolled it and gave Banks, who was still leaning forward, a side-eye. Then grinning sheepishly, he fell back into the backseat, and I unrolled the paper on the armrest. It was a blueprint of the manor and, in detail, explained where everything was.

"My source and buyer says the artifact we're looking for was delivered early this morning. So I can only assume that the professor will want to move it as soon as possible, which means we need to make our move," I told them as we all looked at the blueprint.

"What exactly are we lookin' for again?" Banks asked.

"A sword," I answered. "But not just any sword. Thanatos. Named after Death. It's said that it was fashioned for a god."

"And what makes this sword so valuable?"

"It's made out of pure gold, and the hilt is covered in the rarest of diamonds," I told him and pointed at the blueprint. "There."

"That's the basement," Kelz said. "Is that where you think it will be?"

"A person might assume it would be, but no, I don't think it's there. This is where you would take the hostages after you tie them up if anyone is here."

"Okay, but where do you think the sword is?" he asked.

Although I dropped out of school, I still had access to the campus. And that meant having access to many of the archives. I'd been able to snag an old and recent copy of the manor's blueprint, and what I found was enough to make my heart sing.

"This blueprint was made earlier this year, and why do you think a new one would be made?" I asked and smirked when they didn't answer. "Additions and adjustments to the house. They can often go unchanged, but I'm guessing the professor doesn't have the clearance to do anything without the college knowing since they own the property."

"So what changed?" Banks asked, staring hard at the paper.

"Look," I said and pulled out the copy of the old blueprint so they could compare the two. "Do you see what I see?"

"Yeah, there," Kelz pointed to the closet of the master bedroom. "It looks like he expanded the closet or added another."

"And what would he need two closets for? I took his class. Trust me, the man doesn't need that much space for his clothes," I said. "I think that's a room built inside of his closet. I'll put my money on it that the sword is in there."

"There's only one way to find out," Kelz said, sliding a black mask over his face. "And if necessary, we can have the dear old professor lead the way."

"Uuh, I don't think so," Banks said, pointing ahead at the manor. "Is that your boy right there?"

I followed his finger and saw what he was looking at. It was, in fact, Professor Berkley. He had come out of the tall double doors hastily, wearing a burnt orange suit jacket. A white convertible was parked in front of the manor that he got into and drove off.

"Even better. We have an empty house, fellas," I said with a smile.

When the professor was out of sight, I pulled my own mask down over my face and put on a pair of black gloves. Out of habit, I checked the bullets in my magazine before putting them back in my gun, then put on my backpack. The two of them also grabbed their equipment, and we exited the car, shielded by the night. The best entry point for almost any robbery was the back door of the house, and that was where we headed. We raced through the grass to avoid being spotted by the neighbors, although the houses were spaced widely apart. Once we got to the back, Kelz hopped right to pick the lock on the door.

"You got the jammer, Three?" Kelz asked Banks, using his code name as he worked.

"Just turned it on," Banks said, putting a small device back into his bag. "The alarm system is disabled."

"Good, because we're in," Kelz said, turning the doorknob and gently opening the door.

As he crept inside with his weapon drawn, I covered his six. The area of the home we were entering was dark, and I didn't hear anything. Banks entered after me and closed the door behind him. I pulled out the blueprint again and shined a flashlight on it.

"Okay, we're here," I said in a low voice, pointing at the paper. I darted the light around and figured we were in a sunroom. According to the blueprint, we were right next to the kitchen, next to the foyer and stairs. "We need to go this way."

With confidence, I led the way with my light. We made it through the kitchen, but when we got to the foyer and saw the curved staircase, I got excited and ran to them. The lights suddenly flicked on. At first, I thought Kelz or Banks had done it. However, I froze when I saw that I was staring into the faces of two burly men. The foyer led three ways, and they must have come from the sitting room area. One was an older Latino, and the other was a young, redheaded white man. The fact that they were in the same gray and white getup told me they were security guards. Both were armed and looking at me with wide eyes with their backs to the kitchen.

"What the hell do you think you're doing?" the Latino man asked me, raising his gun.

"Whatever we want to," Kelz's voice sounded, catching them off guard.

Before they could turn around, Kelz had already punched the Latino so hard in his face that he flew to the side. The redhead tried to turn around and get a shot off, but Kelz quickly disarmed him and sent two crashing blows to his ribs. The pain caused him to fall to the floor. I picked up the loose guns and put them in my bag. Moments later, Banks appeared in the foyer from the sitting room, pushing two more guards. Their faces were bloody, letting me know they'd met Banks's fists. He pointed his pistol at the backs of their heads and shoved them forward next to the other two.

"Empty house, huh?" he said from underneath his mask.

"Shut up and go check if there's any more," I instructed.

"I'll do you one better. I passed the control room when I was kicking their asses. I'll go check the cameras."

While he was gone, Kelz and I held down the fort. Finally, after minutes had passed, Banks came back and told us we were all clear. That was all I needed to hear. The guards had been a setback, but nothing we couldn't handle. Still, every extra minute we were inside, the more dangerous the job got.

Kelz unzipped his bag and pulled out a handful of zip ties and duct tape. The Latino had the most fight out of all the men. I saw him preparing to make a move, but the barrel of my gun in his face stopped him.

"Uh-uh, be a good boy. We're not here to hurt any of you," I told them. "So, sit back, relax, and let us do what we came here to do."

"And what's that?" the man asked.

"There's something here that I need. Something very valuable," I told him, and he spat at my feet.

"We won't tell you a thing."

I looked from him to the redhead, who purposely made eye contact with the floor.

"I don't think you'll have to. Tie them up!"

Chapter 5

Nori

Pft! Pft!

The spritz from the Gucci Guilty in my hand hit my wrist and neck. It smelled almost as good as I knew I looked. I glanced at the full-body mirror in my room, taking in my reflection, and smiled at what I saw. My natural shape was one that women all over paid surgeons to get. My breasts sat up nicely in the lace pink pajama top while my bottom ate up the shorts.

Knock, knock.

I grabbed my robe when I heard the knock on my front door and went to answer it. After Nadi left, I tried my hardest to lie down and get some sleep, but it didn't come easy. However, I knew the perfect way to ensure some shut-eye—a good workout.

"Hey," I said with a sly smile when I opened the door.

On the other side of it stood Professor Berkley, my archeology professor. Although well into his forties, he was a handsome and fit man. His father was a white man, but his mother was of both Black and white blood. The mix gave the professor's skin tone a milky complexion. He smiled as his eyes trailed down my body and back to my face.

"You look great," he said back to me, and I stepped out of his way.

He walked into my condo, and I removed his jacket, putting it on the back of one of the bar stools. Unable to help himself, he wrapped his arms around me and grabbed two handfuls of my ass. I tilted my head up just in time to receive his kiss. His tongue swirled around in my mouth like he was trying to figure out what I'd had for dinner.

"Mmm," he moaned after breaking the kiss. "I'm glad you called me tonight."

"I hope I wasn't interrupting anything important," I said, even though I really didn't care if I were.

"Well, I *was* in the middle of intake. I just got my hands on a few delicate relics and was just about to start preparing them for transport. But that can wait."

"Good." I winked and grabbed his hand.

I pulled him like a lost puppy dog into my room and dimmed the lights. Before I could move to remove my robe, he beat me to the punch. After he tossed it to the side, he lifted me in the air and laid me on my bed. As he stepped back and began to undress, I pulled my pajama shorts to the side, revealing that I wasn't wearing any panties, and started playing with my clit.

"I missed her so much," he said, watching me in a trance. "Do you know how much trouble I could get in if the board knew I was fucking one of my students?"

"Does that scare you?"

"Yes."

"Enough to leave this pussy alone?"

"Hell no," he said, dropping his pants and boxers.

Now, some might wonder what I was doing screwing my professor. They might assume I was doing it to get a good grade, but that wasn't it. Plus, I was a great student and averaged a 3.7 GPA. The fact of the matter was that Professor Berkley was charming, and he had a way with the ladies. Not just that, the man was blessed between the legs. I mean, packing that *good* pipe. It was the perfect size, and it was thick. He knew what he was doing with it too. As I rubbed my clit, he stroked his meat until he'd teased himself enough. Then he removed my pajamas and mounted me between my legs.

A hiss escaped my mouth when I felt his wet mouth around my right nipple. He loved my perky breasts and wasn't afraid to show it. His head moved side to side as he gave both of them the attention they needed, and I felt myself get wetter than I already was. I wanted to skip the foreplay and get down to business, but the professor liked taking his time. It was different because, although he didn't like getting head, he loved to give it.

He moved his face between my legs and pushed my legs up and open as far as they would go. Before he dived in, he inhaled a big whiff of my pussy and shuddered in excitement. He first licked from my hole to my clit, and another hiss came from my mouth. That hiss turned into a moan when he began sucking my clit. He was holding my legs so tightly that I couldn't move. I just had to take the pleasure. I gripped the sheets while his mouth made love to me, and I relished the feeling of his tongue flicking over my clit. It didn't take long for my first orgasm to come. I closed my eyes and saw a blinding white light when I erupted into his mouth.

"Oh *fuuuck*," I cried out.

"You ready for me, baby?" he breathed into my pussy.

"Yessss."

On my answer, the professor pulled me to the edge of the bed and stood up. He wiped the juices from his face and rubbed them on his dick before positioning it at my opening. Then he slapped it on my clit piercing a few times before looking me in the face.

"Watch me fuck you," he instructed, and I nodded.

I braced myself, but his thick third leg made me wince every time. He slid inside of me slowly, awakening every sense I had. Once it was in, he ground into me slightly and pulled back to do it again. My back naturally arched as his stroke quickened and had more force. There was nothing like a grown-man dick. One hand held my ankle so he could suck my toes as he was fucking me. The other hand was pinching one of my nipples. My entire body was stimulated, and it felt so good that I almost couldn't take it.

"Professor! Professor! Professor!" I shouted, unable to think of anything else to say.

He was dominating my pussy. And when he flipped me to my side, he showed me who was really the boss. I could hear how wet I was as he pounded in and out of me. My body trembled, and I knew another orgasm was on its way. I didn't stand a chance when he shoved his thumb in my ass as his dick thumped my G-spot. Finally, I couldn't take it anymore, and I let it flow.

"Aaah," I yelled into the air, feeling the stream of liquid try to force him out of my love tunnel.

I think that was what did it for him. His face twisted up like he was in pain, but I knew it wasn't the pain he felt. Instead, it was a raw pleasure. He pulled out of me right before a thick line of semen spilled from his tip and drizzled on my thigh.

"Shit," he shouted as his body jerked. "This pussy is the best. Damn, that was some good shit."

His body jerked again before falling onto my soft bed behind me. I flipped over to face him and watched his chest rise and fall as he caught his breath. I felt powerful, knowing I could take a man's energy like that. It was like I was holding him in the palm of my hand.

"You good, Professor?" I asked with a smirk.

He saw and laughed. Pulling me to him, he kissed me softly on the nose. Out of all the times we'd slept together, that was the first time he'd ever given me butterflies. I pulled my face away the moment I felt them, knowing they would do nothing but get me hurt in the end. What the professor and I had would be left in the bedroom. Nobody could find out about us. If they did, he could be fired, and I could be expelled. So that meant I couldn't afford to catch feelings, and neither could he.

"You want some water?" I asked.

"Please."

"Okay, I'll be right back."

I got up from the bed and left the room to grab him a water bottle. If my legs didn't feel like jelly, I might have skipped. A round two would be lovely, and I hoped he would be up to it after he rested a little bit. However, any hopes of getting taken to Pound Town went out the window when I returned to my room. Professor Berkley was sitting up on my bed with his phone jammed to his ear.

"How the hell did they get in?" he said in an alarmed voice.

He showed no interest in the water in my hand, so I set it on the dresser. Then I grabbed my robe off the floor and put it over my naked body. The look on the professor's face was a mixture of shock and anger as he listened to whoever was on the phone.

"Well, do you know what they took?" Pause. "Shit." Pause. "He's dead? So you mean to tell me there's a motherfucka bleeding on my marble floor right now? Shit, shit, shit! I'm on my way."

He disconnected the phone, jumped up, and dressed in a hurry. It was like I wasn't even there. He pushed past me to get his shoes as I fumbled over what to say.

"Is . . . Is everything okay?" I finally asked.

"No. It's absolutely not okay. Somebody broke into my house tonight and stole a relic," he said angrily. "I was supposed to ship it to a museum in Rome tomorrow. Fuck."

"Somebody . . . died?"

"That's what they're telling me. One of my security guards."

His words made me freeze in shock. Somebody I didn't want to think of crossed my mind. Nadi. I knew she was going on a job tonight, and I couldn't help but wonder if she was the one who had broken into the professor's house. Chills came over me. I wanted to believe it couldn't have been my sister, but I didn't.

Once the professor was fully dressed, he hurried out of the room with me on his tail. When he was confident he had his keys, he opened the front door and left without so much as a goodbye to me. After he was gone, I noticed that he'd left his jacket. I grabbed it and tried to move quickly enough to catch him.

"Professor," I called out when I opened my front door. But I was too late. The doors to the elevator down the hall had just closed. I sighed and took the jacket back inside. Throwing it on the couch, I went back to my room to grab my phone and call my sister. It rang all the way through to voicemail, so I tried again. That time, it didn't even ring. It just went right to her voicemail.

"Oh, Nadi. What have you gotten yourself into?"

Nadi

"If any of you make a move, you'll be dead before you hit the floor."

Behind my mask, my voice was strong and authoritative because I meant every word. The barrel of my Glock was staring at the angry faces of four men who were, unfortunately, at the right place at the right time. I laughed, knowing that they all wanted badly to riddle my body with bullets. And if it were just me standing in the kitchen of the three-story manor, I'm sure they would have. However, on either side of me were two solid, six-foot-plus-sized men. Kelz held an AK-47, and Banks had a machete swinging in both hands. They too wore masks shielding their identities.

As much as I hated to admit it, Kelz was right when he said we didn't need the others. We'd taken the guards' weapons and communication devices. They were defenseless.

As planned, the owner of the manor wasn't present that evening. Our presence had been completely unexpected, so breaking in was easy, as was catching the manor's security off guard. We knew that some security would be present, but nothing we couldn't handle. Now, all we had left to do was get what we came for. Kelz started binding them and duct taping their mouths, but I stepped forward when he got to the last one.

"No, not him," I said. "Give me a second."

While the other guards were glaring at me, I couldn't help but notice that one particular guard hadn't stared our way too long. Instead, his eyes were glued to the floor. In situations like that, one of the smartest things you could do was spot the weakest link. I believed I found him.

"What's your name?" I asked, and when he said nothing, I put my gun to his temple. "I asked you a question."

"Adam," he answered. "I'm Adam."

"Is this your first night on the job, Adam?" I asked him, tapping my weapon on his red hair.

"N-No. First week."

"Ahh, so you *are* fresh. I thought as much." I pulled my gun back and walked around him in a circle, studying him. If I had to guess, I'd say early twenties. Probably had never shot his gun outside of the range. The ring on his finger told me he had someone to go home to. I was smirking by the time I reached his front again. "I'm betting you want to make it back to your pretty wife, don't you?"

"Yes," he answered quickly.

"No matter the cost, right?" I asked, and after hesitating a moment, he nodded his head. "Good. I'm looking for a sword made of pure gold. It dates back to ancient Rome. It's called Thanatos."

"Mmmm," one of the other guards groaned loudly.

I jerked my head his way and fought the snarl that threatened to come to my lips. The man who had made the noise was older. He was still in shape, but the thick gray hair coming from his head and beard gave him away. Kelz and Banks had moved them to one corner of the kitchen and had them kneeling on the ground. The older man's white face had turned red, and he was giving Adam a piercing look. I could only assume he'd been working there for much longer and had a level of loyalty to the manor that Adam hadn't developed yet. Binding and muffling him wasn't enough. I nodded my head at Banks, and he sent the motion back. A second later, he stepped forward and delivered a powerful blow to the man's head. The man fell to the ground, unconscious.

"Now, where were we?" I asked, looking back at Adam. "Oh, that's right, you were about to tell me where Thanatos is."

He glanced over at the other guards. Out of the corner of my eye, I could see them shaking their heads at Adam as if to tell him to keep quiet. I watched Adam's eyes fall on the unconscious man, and he swallowed hard.

"I-I've never heard of it before," he finally said.

"That's disappointing because my very credible source told me that the owner of this house, Professor Berkley, bought it at an auction just last week."

"Maybe your source was wrong," Adam told me, trying to keep a poker face.

"Uh-uh . . . He's never wrong. So—" I cocked my gun and pointed it in the corner where the other men were kneeling. "Either you get to talking, or I squeeze this trigger and hit whoever the fuck I hit. And then . . . you're next. And after that, I will kill your wife for marrying such an idiot. Where is the sword? Five . . . four . . . three . . . two—"

"Okay, okay. Fuck," Adam shouted, holding his palms up. "Shit, I'm going to lose my job over this."

"You'll lose a lot more if you don't talk."

"The sword . . . I saw the professor bring it in last week. It's so heavy that it took two of us to carry it upstairs."

"Legend has it that it was sired for a man with the strength of a god," I said, growing excited. "Where did they take it upstairs?"

"In the professor's bedroom closet, there's a secret door. There's a code. Only he can open the door."

"Except you watched him open the door . . . Didn't you?" I asked, looking up into his face, and he quickly averted his eyes. I knew I was right. I looked at Banks and pointed to the other guards. "Red, you stay down here with them. Blue, come with me."

I called them by their code names since we never called each other by our real names on a job.

"You straight?" Kelz asked Banks before walking away.

"Always."

I shoved Adam toward the kitchen exit and toward the foyer of the luxurious home. We'd been so busy sneaking up on the guards when we first came in that I hadn't even taken the time to notice the brilliant architecture of the place. The wall fortifications inspired by early Roman structures and the high ceilings . . . I particularly liked the contemporary crystal light fixtures throughout the place. They went well with the marble flooring.

I made Adam lead us upstairs to the master suite. Once there, he pointed at a slightly ajar door inside the suite. Not knowing what to expect, I readied my gun just in case I had to use it. Carefully, I crept toward the door and slowly pushed it open. I was met with nothing but what seemed to be endless lines of suits. Flipping on a light switch by the door, I saw that I was staring inside the professor's closet. It was long and wide inside, but at the other end, something was there. It was concealed nicely by the clutter of clothing. However, I had keen eyes. And the first thing I noticed was the overhead light glistening off metal. I got closer and moved the clothes out of the way to get a better look. It was a door like Adam had said. And it was made from some kind of strong metal, titanium maybe. There was no doorknob, only a keypad.

"Bring him here," I instructed Kelz. When he did, I pushed Adam forward and pointed at the keypad. "Open it."

"I don't—we shouldn't . . . I . . . just—" Adam sputtered over his words.

"You just want your wife to die?" I asked. "It won't be hard to learn everything I need to know about you and your entire family. Open the door."

"I only saw him put it in once."

"Then I hope you have a good memory," Kelz said, pointing the AK at his back.

"Okay, okay," Adam said, taking a deep breath and focusing on the keypad.

After staring at it for a few moments, he pressed four numbers. I expected the door to swing open when the last number was input. However, instead of opening, the outer lining of the door turned a bright red.

"That passcode is incorrect. Please try again," an AI woman's voice said loudly.

"You better try harder, Adam," I said, watching sweat beads roll down his freckled face.

"I . . . hold on. Let me think," he said, clenching his eyes shut. "I remember his fingers made an 'X' when he did it. Let me try this."

He input four more numbers, but the door lit up red again.

"That passcode is incorrect. Warning: I will have to alert the authorities if you get the passcode incorrect one more time. Please try again."

"I suggest you get it right this time because if we don't get what we came for, there's going to be a lot of blood to clean up around here," Kelz warned.

Adam looked back at us and then at our guns. He breathed a shaky breath and turned back to the keypad. He concentrated hard on the buttons and put his finger out when ready.

"Three . . . seven . . . nine . . . one," he whispered and closed his eyes as he pressed the last number.

There was a pause, and we all held our breath. I was half-preparing myself to high-tail it out of there. Of course, I would have been angry if I didn't get what I had come for, but empty hands would always be better than being behind a jail cell.

"Access granted," the AI voice said.

Relieved, I felt all the tension leave my body. Shortly after, there was a soft click, and the metal door swung open. I walked through first, and then Kelz dragged Adam through. I was blown away by what I saw. In front of me was a table of golden artifacts. My eyes fell on a pendant on the table. In the center of it was a big rock, a ruby, but not just any ruby. The Sunrise Ruby. And circling the rare stone were black diamonds. My eyes almost bulged out of my head as I looked at it.

"Oh my God," I breathed, stepping forward to look at it closer. "This . . . I think this is the lost medallion of Charlotte DaVinci."

I looked more closely at the carvings in the gold. Then my archaeology studies kicked in, and I remembered learning about the medallion. It was one of a kind, mainly because both stones used to make it were so rare. It dated back to England in the late 1700s when Charlotte was said to have been gifted the medallion by her dying mother, Margarette. Margarette's mother had it crafted for her, and she wanted Charlotte to have it. Maybe to pass it down to her own daughter one day.

However, when Charlotte's father remarried shortly after, the medallion's beauty ignited jealousy inside his new wife. Charlotte's father was as wealthy as they came and had made the most breathtaking necklaces for his new wife. However, she wasn't satisfied. No amount of money could duplicate the medallion around Charlotte's neck. His new wife tried to take it from Charlotte's neck in her sleep, but the girl woke up and fought to keep it. Finally, in a rage, her stepmother strangled her to death with the medallion's gold chain.

Once her treacherous act was found out, the new wife was sentenced to death. And not being able to look at the medallion anymore without feeling the loss of his most dear, Charlotte's father sent the medallion away, never to be found again. That was how the story went, and I always took it for folklore before that very moment. I knew I was holding the real thing in my hands and was lost in a daze by its beauty.

"Black, the sword!" Kelz's voice snapped me back to the moment.

He pointed to the corner of the room where the golden sword leaned against the wall. I forced myself to put the medallion back down and went to the sword. I knelt and carefully examined it. Thanatos was the first of its kind, with a long hilt that had markings of every life it took. The sword in front of me had those very same markings, and from the looks of them, they were very old.

"Is it the real thing?" Kelz asked while my back was to him.

"Oh yeah," I said with a smile. "This is the real thing, all right. We'll live well for a long time off this sale alone."

Staring at it, it didn't look that heavy. However, when I wrapped my hand around the hilt and tried to lift it, it didn't budge. So I tried again with more of my strength and both my hands. That time, it came maybe an inch off the ground.

"He's right," I said. "This thing is heavy. Come get it."

"Aye, you. Carry this with me," Kelz told Adam.

"I don't—"

"Motherfucka, you brought us this far. You think we aren't leaving with what we came for?" Kelz asked.

Adam looked from Kelz to me and nodded. I put my pistol in the holster on my hip and took Kelz's from him. I stepped out of the way and aimed the gun at Adam's back. If he tried something, he was dead.

Kelz grabbed the sword's hilt while Adam was careful not to cut himself with its sharp edge. Then using their strength, they removed it from the professor's secret room. Once they were out, I made to grab the medallion, but the loud sound of a gunshot stopped me. Kelz and I looked at each other before hurrying out of the professor's suite.

With them holding the sword, we couldn't go as fast as I wanted. As we went back down the stairs, all kinds of thoughts were going through my head. Banks had shot somebody. I knew it. We tried our hardest to keep our jobs as clean as possible. In and out on a quick grab, that was it. Nobody usually got hurt. Usually.

When we returned to the kitchen, I froze when I saw the scene. Banks was panting and standing over one of the guards in the corner. A guard was lying motionless at his feet, and Banks was holding a smoking gun. Blood was seeping out everywhere on the floor from a bullet hole in the guard's head. The old man guard had come to while we were upstairs and was staring at Banks in horror. I looked from the body to the still smoking gun in Banks's hand, at a loss for words.

"Red, what the hell is wrong with you?" Kelz asked.

"This motherfucka attacked me," Banks tried to explain, but I felt my brow raise under my mask, mainly because it looked like he had gone over to the guard, not the other way around. The man seemed to have fallen over right where he'd been kneeling. Adam, terrified for his life, dropped the sword and ran off. Banks aimed his gun at his back, but I pushed it down before he could get a shot off.

"You stupid-ass motherfucka. We have a rule. No bodies unless necessary."

"I told you—"

"Fuck what y'all are talking about," Kelz interrupted. "We gotta get up out of here. Now!"

Banks hurried to help Kelz lift the sword, and soon after, we were ghosts in the night.

Chapter 6

Nadi

"Thanatos? You stole Thanatos?"

I thought the high-pitched scream was in my dream for a second, but the violent shake that followed woke me up. Standing next to my comfy California King was my sister glaring down at me. She was dressed in a nice blouse, and the Louis Vuitton messenger bag still on her shoulder told me she was fresh out of class. In her hands, she was also holding a book. I rubbed my eyes and stretched big before sitting up.

The sun shone through the blinds in my bedroom, and when I checked the clock, I saw it read nine in the morning. I would have kicked her if my legs weren't tangled in the sheets. Rest was something my body needed with the days I'd been having, especially since information about the robbery at the professor's manor had hit the news. I could have killed Banks for making us so hot. I didn't know what he was thinking about killing that guard, and I had to make sure Kelz talked to him about that. None of us could afford to go to jail. I rolled my eyes at my sister, wishing she would just leave and let me go back to sleep.

"What?" I asked in an annoyed tone.

"You heard me. You stole the only piece of King Romulus's trio that anyone has found," Nori shouted and pointed at something in the book she was holding.

I realized it wasn't just any book. It was our family's journal. Much of what I'd learned about the world's hidden treasures had come from it. I saw she was pointing at a page dedicated to Romulus and his trio of death. Our great-great-great-grandfather had come face-to-face with the sword many years ago and had documented it. It was how I'd been able to track it down in the first place. I was able to trace every place it had been. Ironically, it ended up in California, making my job easier. I'd done the same for the other two pieces. Knowing I'd used our journal for personal gain and greed, I almost couldn't look Nori in the eye. Almost.

"You're wrong. I found the armor and crown as well."

"You *what?*"

"I found them and sold them. So?"

"So? So? Nadi, *what* are you doing? We weren't given this book to go—to go find its contents like some sort of treasure hunters. We're supposed to *add* to it—not *take* from it."

"And why not?" I asked, throwing off my covers. I would need some water first if I were about to get into a shouting match with her. She followed me out of my bedroom and into our condo's kitchen. "Do you *know* how valuable the things are in that book? I don't see anything wrong with finding a few and selling them to people who will appreciate them."

"Wow. I was only speculating, but you're really using our family's legacy to make a few dollars? I knew . . . I *knew* you were finding things somehow, but this? This is fucking crazy. And you know it."

Blah, blah, blah, blah, I thought. I opened the fridge and was about to grab a water bottle when I saw the expression on Nori's face. I was going to need something stronger. I grabbed a bottle of wine and poured it into a glass. Nori and I were two pieces to the same puzzle, but somehow, we couldn't be more different. After I downed the wine, I turned back to my sister and shrugged my shoulders.

"All these years, we could have been rolling in riches."

"It's not right."

"Well, maybe if Dad would have done what I'm doing, he'd still be alive today," I snapped harshly. "He wouldn't have needed to work a security job

and wouldn't have been murdered. He should've
been . . . He should've been smarter."

"Don't . . ." She paused and jabbed a finger in my
direction. "Don't you talk about him like that."

"I'm just telling the truth. I loved him as much
as you did; still do. But I won't make the same mis-
takes. Do you know why I dropped out of college?
Because there is no better teacher than experience.
While your nose is in the books reading about
adventures, I actually have them."

My words silenced her just like I knew they
would. I put down the glass and made to go to the
bathroom to shower. I let her have the master bedroom because I knew I wouldn't be there as much
as she would. However, we shared the bathroom. I
noticed a jacket on one of the island bar stools on
my exit. It was too big to belong to Nori, and it was
orange—burnt orange. I stopped in my tracks and
turned back to face her.

"Nori, how did you find out about Thanatos?"

My question seemed to catch her off guard. But
she caught herself quickly. She stood up straight
and closed the journal in her hands.

"Professor Berkley was distraught during our
lecture today," she said smoothly. "He said he'd
acquired a rare relic, Thanatos, and had planned
to gift it to a fine arts museum here in Los Angeles.
Unfortunately, however, it was *stolen* before he
could do that."

"Uh-huh," I said, taking another glance at the jacket.

There was a slim chance that the jacket could belong to someone else. However, I couldn't think of anyone else who would wear something so tacky. What had the professor been doing in our condo? I didn't want to think of my sister as a traitor, but she didn't exactly hide the fact that she wasn't happy with me using the journal. I needed to find out more. But until then, I definitely needed to take a shower.

"Nadi?" Nori's voice sounded, and I stopped in my tracks.

"What?"

"This journal was a gift to both of us, but if this is how you're going to use it, then I won't let you have it anymore."

Her words were filled with authority. Sometimes, I felt that she took the fact that she was two weeks older to heart. So, I smiled right before my tongue turned into a needle.

"I guess it's good that I made a copy then," I said, popping her bubble.

Her eyes grew wide before turning into a glare. Satisfied, I once again tried to make my leave. However, she stopped me again.

"Nadi."

"*Whaaaat?*"

"A guard was murdered at the professor's manor the night of the robbery. You're getting sloppy."

Chapter 7

Nadi

After meeting at the hideout, Kelz and I left to meet with Daugherty. He'd flown into town to receive his package and had arranged for us to meet him at the Four Seasons. Usually, I loved getting dolled up and wearing designer clothes, but I wasn't happy that afternoon as I sat in my Chanel dress and heels. There was an elephant in the room, and by the good mood Kelz was in, I was sure he wouldn't address it. Kelz was nodding to a song beating from the speakers, but that stopped when I turned the music down.

"Babe, what are you doing? You know that's my shit."

"You can start it over when I'm done talking," I said, turning to face him in my seat. "We have a problem."

"What? Is it because I nutted too quickly last night? I told you not to do that thing with your ass cheeks. That shit drives me crazy every time," he exclaimed, and I rolled my eyes.

"No, Kelz, be serious. I'm talking about your boy."

"Who, Banks?"

"Yes. He's a problem."

"Man, that was one little body. Be cool, Nadi."

"I can't when he's just killing people in cold blood. We didn't have to catch *any* bodies on that job."

"He said dude charged at him."

"And if that's true, how much damage could he have really caused tied up like that? Banks is a big motherfucka. He could have sat him down with one hit."

"You're overthinking, baby. Are you worried that they will trace the body back to us?"

"No. I'm worried that your friend is getting out of hand. Too much shit is on the line for him to fuck it up. All it takes is one hasty decision—one mistake. You need to talk to him."

"Fine," he sighed. "I'll speak to the man. You happy?"

"No. But I will be when he's in line. And what the fuck is up with Charles and Coney? I hope they know they aren't getting a cut out of this job."

"If Banks decides to put some paper in their pockets from his cut, that's his business. But, yeah. I saw them earlier today."

An uneasy feeling came over me. I couldn't put my finger on it, but there was something about how his jaw clenched and how he hadn't even glanced at me in our conversation. Charles and Coney had been missing for days. Well, at least from me. It was strange that Kelz hadn't mentioned that he'd seen them. He also hadn't told me what was so important that they missed a heist. Was he hiding something?

"Did they take care of whatever they needed to take care of?" I asked.

"Yeah, they got it out of the way."

"And what exactly did they get out of the way?"

"Nothing you need to worry your pretty little head about," Kelz said, finally looking at me.

He flashed his charming smile my way, and usually, it worked to ease my mind. But not that time. I wanted to press the fact because Kelz usually told me everything—I thought, anyway. Without a word, I turned my body back front-facing and stared out the window for the rest of the ride. When we finally reached the hotel, Kelz valet parked the car. While he handed over the keys and got the slip, I got out and made a phone call. It rang twice before it was answered.

"Second floor. Room 243."

Click.

I put my phone back in my clutch as Kelz appeared at my side, holding a case. I fixed his tie right before we walked into the hotel, hand in hand. I smiled at the people who passed us and wondered if they would smile back so cheerfully if they knew a gun was strapped to my thigh. When we made our way inside an elevator, I pressed the number two and stepped back as we went up.

Ding.

"All right, you know the drill," I said as the doors opened. "No money, no deal."

"Let's get this mil then," Kelz said, motioning for me to get off the elevator first.

I winked at him and stepped out, swishing a little harder to make my backside jiggle. Kelz was an ass man, and nothing made him hornier than making money. I couldn't wait to ride him when we were done here. Behind me, he sucked in a quick breath of air through his teeth, and I hoped that meant we were on the same page. I led us to the room and knocked on the door. After a few moments, it opened, and we were ushered inside. Two strong-looking white goons stood by the room's entrance and made to check us for weapons, but I stopped them by holding up a hand.

"If this is meant to be a 'trusting' business transaction, then you won't need to take my gun."

"It is just a precaution," one of them said.

"Then we should disarm you as well," I said, looking him in the eyes.

"Aaah, let them through," a voice called from deeper in the suite.

The men parted and let us pass. We found our way to the suite's kitchen area where Christopher Daugherty sat and sipped brandy. Every time I saw him, I wanted to chuckle. I didn't know if it was the rounded mustache on his pale face or the fact that he spoke with an English accent. I had no idea if he was indeed from Europe, but it was just all so cliché in every sense. He was wrapped in a costly robe, looking like he hadn't left the room all day. His eyes went to the case in Kelz's hand, and he suddenly grew very excited.

"Well, let me see what I'm paying for," he demanded and waved a hand impatiently.

Kelz's jaw clenched, and he looked at me. I shook my head ever so slightly, knowing that he wanted to knock Daugherty off the chair he was sitting on. Instead, he cleared his throat and placed the case on the dining room table. After unlocking it, he opened it and stepped back so Daugherty could examine the sword.

"Oh my word," Daugherty breathed as he stared. "I've never seen anything so beautiful in my life."

From the pocket of his robe, he pulled out an eye loop and examined the diamonds on the sword's hilt. I held my breath. I knew the sword was the real thing, but anything could change the buyer's mind about a purchase. After a few moments,

Daugherty clapped his hands, and I let out the air in my chest.

"Magnificent! I can't believe after all this time, my search for Romulus's lost trio of death is over. It's almost bittersweet," he said as he caressed the sword.

"Where will you take it?" I asked.

"Somewhere safe. Home."

He didn't go into further detail, and I couldn't say I blamed him. As valuable as the artifacts were, I knew he'd only offered us a small portion of their worth. I was sure he would go to great lengths to ascertain no one could find them.

"Well, it's not yours yet," Kelz said seriously. "We've done our part. Now, it's time for you to do yours."

"Right, right. I will send over payment right away," Daugherty said, pulling a phone from his other pocket. He did something on it, and I heard Kelz's phone ding in his pocket. "Done."

Kelz checked his phone to make sure and showed me. As always, Daugherty kept his word. A million dollars was sitting in our account. We smiled at each other, and I nodded at Daugherty.

"It was a pleasure doing business," I said.

"Yeah, stay safe," Kelz said, taking my hand.

We left the same way we entered and went back to the elevator. I stared at Kelz as we waited for it to come up and get us. The Clyde to my Bonnie. There weren't enough words to describe how he made me feel. Especially right then in his suit. The crisp look fit him.

"Have I ever told you how good you look in a suit? I can't wait to get to your place," I said, leaning into him.

He glanced down at me and caught the bedroom eyes I was giving him. The slow grin that came to his face told me that he knew exactly where my thoughts were. The elevator door opened, and I pushed him inside. The sweet taste of his lips felt almost as good as knowing the money was in our account. I felt a strong attraction to him.

"Damn, baby," he breathed when the elevator doors shut behind me.

"Actually. . ." I put my hand down the front of his pants and wrapped it around his growing erection. "Why wait for what I can get right now?"

With my free hand, I reached and pressed the button to stop the elevator from going down. My mouth began to water at the thought of the taste of his flesh, and I fell to my knees. He helped me free his one-eyed monster, and I sighed, satisfied as it stared me in the face. I knew Kelz was excited too by the precum dripping from the tip. He loved when I did spontaneous stuff like that. He especially loved that pleasing him pleased me. I opened my mouth wide and stuck my tongue out before I forced as much of his dick as I could into my mouth.

"Mmmm." The moan wasn't his; it was mine.

My head bobbed back and forth, wetting the monster up more and more with each plunge down my throat. Whenever the head passed my tongue, I swirled it in a circle, causing Kelz to jerk. I sucked fast and then slowed. Fast and then slowed. I would have taken my time if we were at his place, but I knew we didn't have much of that before someone came to check on the elevator. I knew Kelz, which meant I could quickly get him to his climax. I liked letting him think that he controlled the flow in the bedroom, but I really did. Nothing happened until I wanted it to, like right that second. When I wanted him to come, I forced the tip of his manhood to the back of my throat and made a swallow motion like I was trying to force him down. He jerked hard that time, and his body grew rigid as he ejaculated into my stomach. I drank it all up, not leaving one drop before I released him from my mouth.

Looking up at him, I almost laughed at his expression. His eyes were clenched, and his mouth was partially opened as he breathed. He looked like he had eaten something too hot, and if I wasn't mistaken, I could have sworn I saw sweat beads too. His body still trembled, so I took the initiative to tuck him away again and zip up his pants. While he settled into his britches, I pressed a few buttons on the elevator to make it start moving again. I knew after that, he would probably go to sleep as soon as we got to his place, which was fine with me. However, the mall was calling my name.

Chapter 8

Kelz

It wasn't hard to pretend to sleep before Nadi left my condo. Mainly because it was what I wanted to do the most. That girl could pull the nut out of me better than any other woman I'd ever been in. And not only that, but she also wasn't selfish when it came to pleasuring me. Most women only pulled out all the stops if they were getting theirs too. But not Nadi. I think it turned her on to watch what she did to me. To have me in the palm of her hand and feel powerful. She was the only one I'd give that kind of power to. She was a good girl, and I could tell in every fiber of her existence that she loved me and wanted to see me happy. And for that, I trusted her. And that's why it made me feel so bad to know she couldn't trust me.

I waited until I knew she was gone and not coming back to throw the covers back. If I stayed in my comfortable bed any longer, I would go to sleep. And that would be bad for business. So, grabbing my phone, I made a call to Banks.

"You ready?" he asked when he answered.

"Yup. On my way to scoop you right now."

"You got rid of the bitc—"

"Aye, watch your mouth," I snapped, listening to him chuckle on the other end of the phone.

"My bad, man. I forgot you done got tender for her. How the fuck you let that happen anyway? She was just supposed to be a connect that we did away with when we didn't need her anymore."

"Well, we still do need her. Without her, we have nothing. Did *you* know what the hell a Thanatos was before her? Or where to find it?"

"Nah, I failed history class."

"Okay, then. She's helped us become richer men. Respect that. And yeah, maybe I did get tender. For good reason too. You're just mad you ain't get to the pussy before I did."

I said it as a joke, but I knew there was some truth to it. I saw how Banks looked at Nadi sometimes, and I didn't get mad because she was bad as hell. I knew it. That's why I got to it first.

"Yeah, yeah. Whatever, man. Just hurry up. We don't wanna keep Zeus waiting."

He was right about that. We disconnected, and I threw on some more casual clothes. Once my gun was tucked, I left and drove off in my Hellcat. After I picked up Banks, we ditched the car on a piece of land I owned and had turned into a junkyard. There, we switched to a van with tinted windows. With the job we were about to do, we needed something that would easily blend in with any background.

"Let's get this money," Banks said, rubbing his hands together as we drove. "I must admit that you're a genius for coming up with this shit. Selling artifacts and then stealing them back, all to sell them again to Zeus. Ha! And that motherfucka thinks *he's* on top of shit. But really, it's us."

"Hmm," I grunted in response.

There it was—the truth. Charles, Coney, and Banks hadn't been the ones who had talked me into snaking Nadi. I had done that all by myself. See, I was more than a big-time thief before I met Nadi. When Banks and I first got to LA, we used to run money and drugs for Zeus. It was how I scoped out the biggest hits in the city. And since we worked for Zeus, a credible businessman, nobody ever knew it was us. However, when Banks killed the brother of a man named Zayle Heckord, it became apparent that we needed to lay low until the heat got off us. See, Zayle had his hands in Zeus's business in multiple ways. He was both a hired hand and businessman, the perfect general. Killing his brother had been a mistake, and if he ever found out who it was, we were as good as dead. Thankfully, shortly after that, I met our next lick. Nadi.

I didn't plan to catch feelings for her. At first, she was just a girl who liked to go on treasure hunts. I thought she was crazy at first. It all sounded like some *National Treasure* bullshit to me. But then she showed me that it was real. And she also showed me how lucrative these hunts could be if we not only found things but also sold them. Our first find was a diamond necklace dating back to the 1700s. It was around a white woman's neck then, and Nadi was happy to see it. But I wanted it, and Nadi wanted me. It was our first heist together, if it could be called that. It wasn't hard to snatch it from the woman's neck. It also wasn't hard to talk Nadi into continuing to sell the things we found, not when the money came pouring in. I brought Banks, Charles, and Coney in on it; the rest was history.

That was two years ago. Back then, Nadi was just a check to me. She was a means to a means. But the more I got to know her, the more I liked her. And then that like turned to love, but I didn't think I'd be able to love anyone as much as the green, which was why I came up with a way to make more.

Banks continued talking my ear off, but I didn't hear a word he said because I was too lost in my memories.

Ding.

After I pressed the doorbell to the mansion, I stepped back, feeling the weight of the duffle bag in my hand. I looked to both sides of the tall double doors at the guards standing there watching me like a hawk. I assumed they weren't allowed to leave their posts, or else I was sure they would have walked me in. When one of the doors finally opened, a woman I'd come to know as Kiara opened the door. She was a gorgeous, dark-skinned woman with locs, and she was off-limits, which was why I hated when she eyed me with her flirtatious eyes.

"Kelz."

"Hey, Kiara. How are you doing?"

"I'm good, but you should be able to tell that by looking at me," she said, running her hands down her curves. "Come in. Zeus is expecting you."

"I would hope so. This is his money," I said, holding up the bag, and she stepped back so I could walk in.

"Well, now we know he'll surely be happy to see you. Come on. You can wait in the sitting room while he wraps up with Zayle."

She took me to a big room decorated elegantly. It was funny that it was called the sitting room because it looked like a room a person wouldn't want someone to sit in at all. Still, I popped a squat on the pale couch, careful not to hit the crystal lamp on the glass table beside it on the way down. Tall windows gave me a nice view of the property's garden, but I didn't care to look at it.

"Zayle's here?" I asked Kiara before she left, trying not to sound suspicious. "Why?"

"Business, I'm sure." She shrugged with her hand on her hip. "That bastard doesn't even speak when he walks through those doors anymore. That's why I like you. Your mama raised you right. But then again, Zayle hasn't been right since those motherfuckas killed his brother, Zaire."

"Yeah, I heard about that," I said, shaking my head like it was a shame. "They figure out who did it?"

"I don't think so. But let me get you some water or something while you wait. No telling how long they'll be in the office."

When she was gone, I let out a breath of fresh air. I was relieved that nobody knew about my involvement in Zaire's murder. I might not have been the one who pulled the trigger, but in Zayle's eyes, I would be just as much to blame, especially since the murder took place in Zayle's own house.

It was supposed to be an in-and-out job. One thing I'd learned by running for Zeus was that wealthy men were idiots with a god complex. They all kept a safe of valuables in their home because, for some reason, they thought it was the safest place. Zayle was no different.

On a night that I knew he would be gone doing a banquet event honoring Zeus's commitment to the community he'd come from, Banks and I made our move. We didn't know that Zayle had sent his brother back to his house to grab the gift he planned to give Zeus that evening. We were wearing masks and could have easily knocked Zaire out cold, finished the job, and left. But Banks got beside himself. When Zaire entered the room and we saw who he was, Banks didn't hesitate to shoot him. I will never forget the vision of his head snapping or his body dropping to the floor. It was in cold blood and unnecessary. Zaire had been unarmed.

"Kelz." The voice jerked me out of my memory.

Turning my head, I saw Zeus standing in the room with me, but he wasn't alone. Zayle was with him. He had the hard look of someone who had seen things nobody talked about. I avoided his eyes and, instead, focused my attention on Zeus. I stood up and grabbed the bag I'd brought with me.

"I brought this for you," I said, holding up the bag.

"What's that?"

"One guess. It's green with dead people on it."

"My boy," Zeus exclaimed and patted me on the back. "I wasn't expecting this drop until Friday."

"Yeah, well, it's Tuesday, and I have a way of ensuring people pay their dues early. I think they're trying to suck up to you."

"Or maybe you are," Zayle said, breaking his silence.

I clenched my jaw and turned to face him. I'd felt so much empathy toward him for his loss that I'd almost forgotten what a pain in the ass he was. The way he was looking at me, it was like I was beneath him. I wondered what his expression would change to if he knew that the chain around my neck was bought with the money I'd stolen from his safe.

"I don't suck up to anybody. I do, however, know how to do my job effectively," I told him evenly.

"That's not surprising. All dogs know how to fetch."

His words made me step toward him, but Zeus, who had been watching the exchange with an amused look, placed his hand on my chest.

"Put the swords away, gentlemen," he said but raised his brows in my direction.

"My bad," I said, and Zayle just grunted.

"I will see you tomorrow, Zayle," Zeus said, and Zayle nodded.

He gave me one last distasteful look before leaving the room. Then in the distance, I heard one of the front doors open and knew he was gone. Zeus waved for me to follow him to his office, and I did, bag in tow.

"Sit," he instructed once we were there.

He sat behind his desk, and I sat on the opposite side, placing the duffle bag on top. He pulled it to him and began rummaging through it. As he did that, I took the time to look around his office. It wasn't my first time inside it, but it seemed to accumulate something new each time. Last time, it was the golden vase sitting at the edge of his desk. That time, it was the painting on the wall. It was new to his office, but it wasn't new to the world. The paint looked old, almost as if it had faded over time. That, or it had been painted a lifetime ago, during the Renaissance era perhaps. My girl, Nadi, had taught me a thing or two about spotting that kind of thing.

"I didn't take you for a lover of the arts," I said, pointing at the painting. "If I had to guess, I'd say Crivelli."

"And I'd say you would be right." Zeus stopped counting the money to give me his attention. He seemed impressed. "And yes, I do love the arts,

especially the rare ones. That painting alone is worth more than the car I drive. People pay unimaginable amounts of money for art and relics, myself included. Something most don't know about me is that I'm a collector and a seller."

"I guess there is more to you than meets the eye."

"Take these words and hold them near. There's more to everyone than meets the eye. See, when people look at me, they see a philanthropist, a drug dealer, or a monster. Not someone with a hobby as lucrative as mine. Everybody can do good deeds and sell drugs, but not many can say they've ever touched an ancient artifact, let alone owned one. It's addictive. You may find out one day."

"Actually, we may have more in common than I ever thought," I said, unable to keep my thoughts to myself. My mouth seemed to have a mind of its own.

"Do tell."

"One of my side hustles is treasure hunting. I've been doing it for years," I told him, which was partially true. Minus the "for years" part.

"And what all have you found?" Zeus asked, not caring to hide the curious look on his face.

"The lost diamonds of Leaunna," I told him and watched his brows raise.

"That's been lost for—"

"Centuries, I know. And my buyer paid a pretty penny for it," I told him.

"And how did you get your hands on such an item?"

"I have a team," I lied with ease. It really sounded like I knew what I was talking about. Like I hadn't just learned about most of it in the recent months, but he didn't know that. I gave him a small smile and continued to yank his chain. *"Working for you is all right, but I can see myself out of the game for good now. You were right when you said people pay unimaginable amounts for rarities and relics. It makes running the streets seem like a cotton field if you know what I mean."*

"I understand what you mean," Zeus said, leaning back and tapping his fingers together.

What are you doing? *I asked myself in my head. I was dangling myself in front of Zeus's face, hoping he would bite. I couldn't tell if I had offended him. He had pointed out the road, so I walked down it.* Please don't let this man kill me, *I thought. But no, he didn't kill me. Instead, he smiled.*

"I think I might have another use for you, Kelz. That is if you and your team pass the preliminaries."

When I came back to reality, Banks was still talking. He hadn't even realized that I'd checked out for a while. As I listened to his voice, I wondered if I had made a mistake by bringing him on board when Zeus put his offer on the table. It just seemed like the right thing to do at the time. Putting your people on was the law where I came from. I just felt like if I was making a bigger bag, then why not let him in on it? But I should have considered what he had done to Zaire before I did so. And now, he had killed someone in what was supposed to be a clean in and out.

"A few more jobs and we'll all be millionaires. I told my punk-ass grandma I would be rich someday," Banks said.

I glanced over at him and saw that he had a dopey smile. I wished I could smile with him, but Nadi was right. I had to address the issue at hand.

"Aye, yo, Banks. You okay?"

"Yeah, why would you ask that?"

"I don't know. You just fucked me up at the last job by killing that man."

"I told you, he attacked me," Banks said forcefully.

"It looked to me like he was tied up in the spot we left him in," I said, watching his body language out of the corner of my eye.

He was quiet. I could see his fist clench and unclench. I'd known Banks for a while, and I also knew that he could have a temper on him. But I never thought it was something I couldn't handle.

"Is that right?" he finally said.

"Yeah. So, tell me what really happened."

"I told you already."

"I mean the *real* story, Banks. Why did you kill that man? The shit made the news. I only have one rule: no mess unless necessary."

"Okay, you want the real story? He looked at me funny."

"He looked at you funny?" I wasn't sure I had heard him right.

"You heard me," he clarified. "My trigger finger itched, and I scratched it. That's all there was to it."

"Come on, Banks. You know better."

"I *know* better? Are you my daddy now? Because last I checked, that asshole has been dead for ten years."

"You know what I mean. I brought you into this shit."

"Yeah, you did. I'm glad, you know. So that way, when Zeus finds out we've been doubling up on payments, he'll know exactly who to blame. And what about that fine bitch of yours? I'm sure she'll be happy to learn you've been playing her all this time."

I was shocked not only by his words but also by the fact that he would even use those two things against me. He was wrong to kill the man at the professor's house, and after learning the reason, I was convinced he just had a taste for blood. I almost didn't recognize the man in the passenger seat. He smirked over at me like he knew he had me in a tight spot, but my next words wiped away that same smirk.

"I wonder what Zayle will do when he finds out who was responsible for his brother's death."

I almost felt a chill coming across me in the car when the words were out. We hadn't talked about the incident since it happened. But he knew just like I knew how serious the act was. When I glanced at him again, his eyes were empty.

"You wouldn't say shit. Not when you were there too."

"Says who?" I asked, mimicking his smirk. "I was wearing a mask, and unlike you, I liquidated everything we got from that safe. You sitting there wearing the motherfucka's watch and shit. Stupid."

"That's low, dog."

"You set the bar," I reminded him and then sighed. "This is petty. You know I'm not going to say shit. Just like I know you aren't going to say shit. Right?"

"Right," he said, exhaling forcefully.

"A'ight then. All I'm trying to say is if we want the money to keep coming in, we have to be clean. What we're doing is next level. Nobody in the streets is getting money like us. So let's keep it this way."

"I hear you."

Those were the words that left his mouth, but his stony expression said something else. I felt like I was driving with a stranger in the car, not a man I considered my brother. Every piece of my being was screaming at me to cut him out. My gut told me that giving him another chance was a mistake, but even though he didn't feel like my brother then, it didn't change the fact that he was. So just like that, my anger faded away like breath on a mirror.

We were almost at the same Four Seasons Hotel that Nadi and I had left earlier that day. Before I got there, I pulled out my phone and called. The person who answered the other side was a woman.

"Hello?"

"Pamela, we're almost there. Do your thing."

"Got it."

Pamela was one of Zeus's girls. I guessed when a person was as rich as him, he could afford to have multiple women who lived together harmoniously. And none of them had a problem getting their hands dirty for him. At that moment, Pamela was jamming every camera in the hotel. Five minutes later, I felt my phone vibrate. It was her.

Ready. You have thirty minutes.

"Showtime," I said.

Chapter 9

Zeus

The white of my teeth was probably blinding when Christopher Daugherty opened the door to room 243. The shock on his face when he saw me brought a shiver of pleasure to my spine. He didn't know who I was, but his step backward told me what I already knew about my presence. I was to be feared. I laughed as his eyes darted to Kelz in confusion. I understood, of course, since that was the face he'd seen when he peered through the peephole. I thought it would be best since Kelz had been the point of contact for the sale. Or what was supposed to be a sale. However, I only planned to make one payment, which would go to the people with me. Usually, I didn't show up for the acquisition of items, but that time, I wanted to be present. Kelz and his partner Banks had rushed into the room and disarmed Christopher's security guards before they could draw their weapons.

"*Oof!*" one of them grunted when Kelz crashed his fist into the side of his head.

As he fell to the ground, so did the other, courtesy of Banks. Christopher's mouth moved, but no sound came out. I stepped inside and let the door shut behind me. A smile crept to my face as I looked past Christopher at three boxes on a couch. They all varied in size, but one was notably larger than the others. The dolly nearby told me he was soon about to transport them out.

"What is the meaning of this?" Christopher demanded to know.

"Business," Kelz replied.

"Business, you call it. This isn't how I conduct business," Christopher shouted. "I just pai—"

"You win some, you lose some." Kelz interrupted him before he could finish.

If looks could kill, Kelz would have dropped dead where he stood. So it was a good thing they couldn't. The daggers Christopher shot from his eyes were just as harmless as the men meant to protect him, currently snoring on the ground. I stepped toward the couch, and Christopher tried to block my way. Banks snatched him by his arm and put a gun to his dome. He couldn't do anything but watch. When I got to the first box, my heart rate quickened with excitement.

"You and I have much more in common than you know, Christopher," I said, gripping the top of the box.

"I don't even know you. And even if I did, I doubt we would be anything alike."

"Oh, but we are. See, I have a taste for fine things too."

"Yeah, right. You have no idea what's in those boxes or how valuable they are," he spat.

"You'd be surprised at how much I know. I know exactly what these boxes hold. For a long time now, I've been in search of the three lost treasures of King Romulus. Do you know they say the person who wields all three would be powerful beyond any man's wildest dreams?"

I lifted the lid and feasted my eyes on the beauty before me. It was the crown of King Romulus, and it was beautiful. The jewels in it glistened in the light like morning dew on the grass. I removed the tops of the other boxes and couldn't shake the giddy feeling. There was nothing like owning something that was only made once, and that was the case for each item before me.

"Hhh-hey! Those are mine. Get your paws off," Christopher shouted.

"Correction. They *were* yours," I told him. "But honestly, I must say, it's almost too good to be true. You, the holder of all three, bringing them here of all places. Together. The museum you were selling them to must have been paying a hefty price."

"Museum?" Christopher asked with a gasp. I looked up just in time to see Christopher's eyes widen in horror. "Why, I would nev—"

I stopped listening to him talk when my phone rang. I wouldn't have answered it if it weren't Pamela's ringtone. I hurried to respond.

"Are we still good?"

"Yeah," she answered in her sexy voice. "The cameras are still jammed. Nobody is panicking."

"Good. How are we doing on time?"

"You're closing in on fifteen minutes, baby," she told me.

"We'll be gone before then," I said, hanging up and putting the lids back on the boxes. I looked at the men on the ground and then up at Kelz. "Kill them, and then help me get this shit out of here."

"What about him?" Banks asked, nudging Christopher.

At that point, all the blood drained from Christopher's face. Even he knew what was about to happen to him. I didn't know why Banks had asked such a stupid question.

"We don't have masks on, do we?" I asked.

"Nah."

"Okay, then. You know what to do, or do I need to instruct you?"

Kelz already had the silencer on his gun. Without hesitation, he approached the two men on the floor and shot them point-blank in the head. The thing about him that I'd always liked was that he never killed unless he had to. I rarely ever had to send a cleaner team to tidy up his messes. He got in and out. But that job was different. We wouldn't have been able to walk into the building without raising the alarm if we wore masks. Christopher had seen all our faces. We didn't have a choice.

"I should have never trusted you," Christopher said, looking at Kelz.

He was taking things very personally, and I couldn't help but notice a flash of guilt cross Kelz's face. I could have been wrong, but that was what it looked like. Christopher opened his mouth to say something else, but by then, Banks had put lead into the back of his neck and skull. He was dead before he hit the ground.

We put the boxes on the dolly and pushed the artifacts out of the room. When we returned to the hotel lobby area, many people were around. But the good thing about rich people was that they were usually too self-absorbed to notice the things happening around them. We pushed the dolly outside and loaded the artifacts into the back of my Cullinan with five minutes to spare. And by the time the cameras finally began operating again, we were already gone from the property.

Chapter 10

Nori

The sound of my alarm clock obnoxiously going off let me know it was time to get up for class that morning. If it weren't for my ambition, I would have turned it off and gone right back to sleep. But of course, I didn't do that. Instead, I got up and hit the shower. I chose a nice taupe legging set and a pair of white sneakers when I got dressed. I had Professor Berkley's class that morning and wanted to be effortlessly cute. After putting my hair in a bun and slaying my edges, I grabbed the designer backpack Nadi gifted me to make up for stealing the sword. I was still upset with her, but a bigger part of me was upset with myself. I was a hypocrite. I couldn't scold her for the path she was on if I was willingly reaping the rewards. I could tell her to stop because it went against what we stood for. However, I also wasn't willing to give up the lifestyle. I wasn't ready to cut ties with my sister. She was my best friend and the most loyal person I knew. I would have to find a way to come to terms with things.

I left my room and prepared to depart. However, a big mound on the living room couch stopped me. The closer I got to it, I realized it wasn't a mound. It was Nadi wrapped in a blanket. She was knocked out with her mouth open, and before I shook her awake, I pulled my phone out to take a picture. Right when I was about to snap, her eyes flipped open wide, and I jumped back with a squeal.

"Why are you taking pictures of me while I'm sleeping?" she asked in a groggy voice.

"Because you're the cutest troll I've ever seen," I teased and put my phone away. "If it makes you feel better, I didn't get the shot because you woke up looking like the demon in *The Exorcist*."

Nadi sat up and stretched her arms wide while yawning. I noticed that she was still dressed in her street clothes, which was something she rarely did, not unless she was exhausted. Rubbing her eyes, she grabbed her phone and got up from the couch. Her first stop was in the kitchen to pour a glass of orange juice. I glanced at the front door, knowing that if I didn't leave right then, I would be late for class, but something told me to stay. Maybe it was the disturbed expression she had on her face as she scrolled through her phone. Or the fact that she didn't take one sip of the juice she'd just poured.

"You good?" I asked, and she looked up at me as if suddenly remembering I was there.

"It's . . . nothing," she said and sat down on one of the bar stools.

"Then why are you looking like something is bothering you?"

"I said it's nothing, Nori."

"Uh-huh," I said, watching her continue staring at whatever was on her phone. "I guess I'll just have to see for myself."

Quickly I plucked the phone from her hand and blocked her so she wouldn't be able to take it back.

"Nori!"

I ignored her and thwarted all her efforts to get her phone back while I read a news article she had pulled up on her phone.

Two weeks ago, the body of millionaire Christopher Daugherty was found in the suite he was staying in at the Four Seasons Hotel. The day investigators believed the murder happened, the hotel experienced a malfunction with its cameras. No leads have been made at this time.

I stopped reading, trying to determine why it bothered Nadi so much. I focused on the name of the murdered man. "Christopher Daugherty. Daugherty. Why do I feel like I know this name?"

"Because you do," Nadi sighed and finally took her phone back. "It's in the journal. Not Christopher Daugherty, his great-grandfather, Leonard. Grand-dad Giovanni wrote about him. He was some sort of great collector. A hobby he obviously passed down to Christopher."

"And why do you seem so butt hurt about him being dead?"

"Because . . . because I saw him that same day."

"Excuse me?" I raised my brow.

"Christopher is who hired us to get the sword. We dropped it off to him that day."

"We, as in you and Kelz?"

"Yeah."

"Nadi, please don't tell me you—"

"I'm not a monster, Nori. I'm not a saint, either, but I wouldn't kill anyone in cold blood."

I could tell that I hurt her feelings, so I backed off. Also, it was apparent that she was really distraught over it all. So I sat on a bar stool beside her and looked into her face.

"So, it's safe to assume that whoever did this now has the sword since they didn't report finding it."

"That's not all."

"What do you mean?"

"That wasn't the first time Christopher had hired us. There were two more times before that. Nori . . . Christopher had all three of King Romulus's lost treasures in that suite."

"*Nadia,*" I groaned.

"I know, I know. It's a crazy coincidence," she said, but there was a hint of doubt in her voice, and I knew why.

"It's a hell of a coincidence if you ask me. For him to be murdered right after he got all three treasures? And I'm sure he wasn't broadcasting his exact location. Someone had to have known."

"The only people who knew about anything were me and my team."

"How well do you really know them? Kelz included. Stop thinking with your heart and pussy and think with your head, Nadi."

"Kelz wouldn't do something like that." She shook her head ferociously. "He wouldn't double-cross me. And he wouldn't betray my trust."

"Why? Because he loves you?"

"Yes," she exclaimed, jumping up.

"Prove it."

"Prove what? That he loves me?"

"No. Prove that he wouldn't cross you. All of the people who have hired you, look them up right now."

Nadi hesitated at first. I didn't know if it was because I was challenging her or because she was afraid of what she might find. Eventually, she just walked away and went to her room. I shook my head and prepared to head out, but she returned with a laptop and sat down.

"Fine," she said and opened a search engine.

"Who are you looking up?" I asked, facing the laptop.

"Margarette Pine. We sold some rare jewels to her two months ago in Georgia," she answered and clicked on an article.

Renowned philanthropist Margarette Pine was found stabbed to death in her Georgia residence earlier this evening.

"Oh my God."

"Check the date."

"February twentieth," she breathed. "That's three days after we made the delivery. I remember when we got back, Kelz left again. He said he and Banks had to go out of town again on business. I didn't think . . . I didn't know . . ."

"Look up another one."

"Okay."

She typed in the name Taylor Sherfield, a man who resided in New Mexico. He was also found dead shortly after Nadi and her crew dropped off their items. I let her search a few more names before making her stop because her fingers were trembling.

"Nadi . . ."

"Why would he do this? Why would he betray my trust?"

"Isn't it obvious? The kind of items you find and sell never lose their value. They need you to find them in the first place. Once you do, you sell them to whoever hired you, right?"

"Right."

"After that, Kelz and the others don't need you anymore. They know exactly where the items are now, so why not steal them and sell them again? They're getting a double payday. I'm just going to say it. Your team? Terrible businessmen. So much for the term 'honor amongst thieves.'"

"I should have listened to you about Kelz. He was just using me." The sadness in her voice was slowly turning into anger.

I recognized the look of rage on her face and reached out to her, but it was too late. She moved quickly from my grasp and stood up. Light flashed off her gun on her waist, and she started for the door. I tried once again to stop her.

"Nadi, where are you going?" I asked.

"To handle my business."

Seconds later, the front door opened and closed. She was gone. I didn't know what she planned to do to Kelz, but it couldn't have been good. I could have run after her and talked some sense into her, but I didn't. Kelz deserved every bit of wrath he had coming his way. So instead, I grabbed my bag and left, hoping to still make it to class.

***

Traffic was not on my side that morning, but I could still make it to campus with thirty minutes left of class. I hurried to Professor Berkley's room to catch the tail end of his lecture, but to my surprise, the room was empty of students. I checked my watch to make sure I had the correct time.

The professor sat at his desk, his head leaning back and his eyes closed. He must have let the class leave early. Instead of being annoyed that I had darn near run from the parking lot to the archeology building, I decided to make the most of the alone time the professor and I now had. I'd always fantasized about making love in the classroom.

I crept down the steps to his desk, careful not to make any noise to alert him I was there. However, the closer I got, the more I heard a distinct slurping sound. It also became apparent that the professor wasn't sleeping. His mouth was slightly open, and soft moans were coming out. It didn't take a rocket scientist to figure out what was happening. The only thing left to see was what other college girl he was dealing with. When I got close enough, I was mortified to see whose lips were wrapped around his dick, sucking the life out of it. And it wasn't a woman at all.

"Professor?" I gasped in disgust.

Professor Berkley's eyes snapped open, looking at me in horror. He pushed the man away from him and jumped up, frantically trying to put his dick back into his pants. The man stood up too, and I stared at him, taking in his tight pink jeans and a scarf around his neck. I couldn't believe it. The professor was down low. My body reacted without me telling it to as I began to back away.

"Nori. It . . . It isn't what it looks like," he pled with me.

"So, I wasn't just suckin' that dick?" the man said flamboyantly, jerking his neck.

"Shut up, Edmund," the professor shouted.

"No. I'm not about to let you keep fucking me whenever you please, just for you to treat me like trash right after."

I couldn't take any more. I turned and ran up the stairs. I was glad I hadn't eaten anything that morning because I for sure would have thrown it up. I had nothing against gay people, but I couldn't stand a man who couldn't live in his truth. I was a straight woman who wanted a straight man. I stopped to catch my breath when I was out of the classroom and halfway down the hallway.

"Nori!" the professor's voice sounded right behind me, and I whipped around to face him. He must have run after me. "Please, Nori. It isn't what it looked like."

"Then what was it? Because I'm pretty sure you were just letting another man please you."

"I'm just . . . I'm just under a lot of stress, and he was there. That's all. I needed something to ease the tension. I'm not gay."

"A straight man wouldn't let another man suck his dick just to ease some tension, Professor."

"As I said, I'm under a lot of fire by the Collector Society. The museum paid them a lot of money for the safe transport of an item in my possession. It was stolen when my home was burglarized. You don't understand what this means for me."

I didn't know in what world he thought the two scenarios correlated, but he could go right back to that one. Matter of fact, he could have gone straight to hell. I heard what the man said as I ran out of class. They'd been sleeping together for a while now, which meant he was sleeping with both of us at the same time. I knew I had to get out of there before I hurt him badly.

"You have me so fucked up right now. How could you? You know there are all kinds of monsters in this world, but men like you are the worst. I can't *stand* a down low motherfucka!"

"I'm not gay," he insisted.

"Fuck you. I bet you won't do this to another woman again, *especially* a Black woman."

"What is that supposed to mean?" he asked, suddenly turning dark. "You can't expect to tell anyone about what you saw here today."

"You'll see," I said and turned my back on him to walk to the building's exit.

"Bitch, you won't be saying a word. This won't be the first time I had to get rid of a problem," he growled and gripped my shoulder tightly.

I grabbed him by the wrist and tossed him over my shoulder like he didn't weigh more than a sack of potatoes. He landed hard on his back and groaned in great pain. It was split-second muscle memory and using his weight against him. The moment I sensed I was in danger, all the training instilled in me came rushing back. I placed my foot on the professor's neck and applied pressure, causing him to gasp for air.

"Trust me when I say I'm *not* one you want to fuck with," I said, glaring down at him.

Right before he passed out, I removed my foot, allowing him to breathe again. I heard the screams of the man the professor was involved with and knew it was time to go. Not home, though. I didn't want to be alone. There was only one place that could ease my mind.

Chapter 11

Nadi

"No honor amongst thieves."

Nori's words played over and over in my head as I burst through the front door of Kelz's place. There was no calming the storm brewing in my chest. He had lied to me and manipulated me. I was more than just embarrassed that I had allowed myself to be used in such a way. I slammed the door behind me and shouted at the top of my lungs.

"Kelz! Kelz! Where the fuck are you?"

He came rushing from the master bedroom, gun in hand. The look on his face was a bewildered one as he looked around, no doubt trying to find the cause for the alarm . . . unknowing that it was him.

"Baby, what's wrong?" he asked with wide eyes. "You good? You were shouting like someone was trying to kill you."

There was concern in his eyes that I wanted to slap away. The nerve. How could he even look me in the eye, knowing what he was doing in the background? Snaking me must have become like second nature to him. He didn't even feel it anymore. It was just a way of life.

"How could you?" I asked, feeling the fire in my gaze.

"How could I *what?*" he asked, confused.

"You know what!"

"I really don't, baby. Come lie down. You look like you could use some rest. And are these the clothes you had on yesterday?"

He tried to grab my arm and lead me back to the bedroom, but I removed myself from his grasp. When he turned to face me again, it was my phone screen that he was looking at. I was holding up the same article Nori had read earlier. The look on his face changed from confusion to guilt, and just like that, I knew my suspicions were correct. My heart fell into the pit of my stomach, and I let my hand drop.

"Nadi . . ." He took a step toward me.

"Don't touch me. Stay the fuck back. I can't believe this."

"Nadi, please, listen."

"How long?"

"Baby, if you'll just let me explain—"

"How long have you been doing this shit behind my back?" I shouted, and he sighed.

"It's been awhile. A really long while."

My hand went to my chest. His words were like a physical blow of pain that I could feel. As I stared at him, I felt tears come to my eyes, knowing that whatever we had was done at that moment. There was no coming back from that kind of betrayal.

"I defended you. Whenever Nori said you were no good, I stuck up for you. For *us*. When she said you were using me, I swore to her that you weren't—all to find out that you were the whole time."

"I never used you, Nadi. Not intentionally."

"And that's better?"

"No. No, it's not," Kelz said, setting his gun on the dining room table. He ran his hands over his face in defeat. "I guess it's time to tell you the truth."

"You think? You've killed people who *trusted* me."

"We didn't kill all of them—only those who saw our faces. You know the game, Nadi. And money is the biggest part of it. When Zeus let it be known to me that he was a collector of the kind of treasures we can find, I couldn't pass up the opportunity. Especially knowing for a fact that he could pay the fee."

"Zeus?" I asked, recognizing the name of the biggest kingpin in California. "When did you start working for Zeus?"

"For almost as long as I've been in Cali."

"So, what? He waits for you to steal back what you've sold and then pays you for it? That doesn't make any sense. I couldn't see him paying top dollar knowing you've already been paid for—wait," I stopped myself midsentence and widened my eyes. "He doesn't *know* you're getting paid twice, does he?"

"No."

"Do you *know* what he'll do to you if he finds out? Zeus isn't a man to play with, Kelz."

"I know, which is why he'll never find out."

I never knew him. I was the kind of person that held a lot of myself back, but what I *did* put out were genuine pieces of me. They were just the ones I felt comfortable willingly giving. The rest of the pieces had to be earned. Kelz had earned them with the fake pieces of himself, and that was the toughest pill to swallow. I was looking into the face of a stranger.

"You better believe he'll never find out because I'm done," I spat. "No me, no treasure. You, Banks, and the rest can go back to robbing dope dealers. Kiss my ass."

I turned to go, but he caught my hand. With my free one, I turned around and delivered a loud smack to the side of his face. He was stunned that I'd hit him and even more stunned when I delivered a second slap.

"I hate you. You've broken my trust and heart with decisions you knew would make me feel like this. You chose to do them anyway. You're a liar and deserve to be in the hottest part of hell. This isn't what I signed up for, and I won't let my great-grandfather's journal have any more unnecessary blood tied to it. We're over. If you *ever* contact me again, I'll kill you."

I managed to turn away from him just in time so he wouldn't see my hot tears fall. I held my sobs in until I left and made it back into my car. And even then, I held them in when they were screaming to come out. The fallen tears were all that he would get. He wasn't worth my pain. Still, I felt like a lost puppy, and there was only one place to go.

Home.

Chapter 12

Nori

The kitchen of my childhood home was quiet, minus the sound of my spoon scraping the last of the smothered chicken and rice off my plate. Everyone was partial to their parents' cooking, but my mom could really throw down. In high school, my friends all but begged to come home with me for dinner almost every night. As filling as the smothered chicken was in my stomach, it didn't heal the soreness in my heart.

What I'd witnessed at the school campus still played like a movie in my head. It would be almost unbelievable if down-low men weren't so common in society. The crazy thing to me was that I had experienced it personally. I probably would have never found out if I had not seen it with my own two eyes. Although the professor and I weren't publicly in a relationship, we'd often gone on dates. I couldn't help but wonder if any of the men he was dealing with were in any of the places we were . . . If any of them were laughing at me not knowing the truth about him. It was sick that any man would put a woman through that. Even sicker that he took away my choice.

"What's got you in such deep thought?"

The sweet sound of my mom's voice brought me back to the current moment. She was standing over me, giving me a motherly eye. No matter how long she had lived in California, she still had that North Carolina accent. I realized I'd been gripping my spoon tight and staring at my plate. I didn't know if I'd even blinked. Dropping my spoon, I pushed my plate from in front of me so I could rest my arms on the table. I opened my mouth to tell her, "Nothing," but I hated lying to her. So instead, I just shrugged my shoulders.

"Mm-hmm," she said, taking my plate to the sink.

The cute dress she wore clung to the hourglass shape she'd maintained since I was a child. In fact, my mom had barely aged in my eyes since then. She was in her mid forties, but looked much younger than that. Many assumed her black would crack when my dad was found dead. They thought she couldn't keep going, but she had a reason to keep going. Her girls. She couldn't lose herself in grief because then, we would have lost two parents. So she mourned her lost love in our faces and out.

But that sadness turned into acceptance. Life must always go on. She had made one change, though. She cut her hair into a pixie cut and wore it like that ever since. It brought out her high cheekbones and doe eyes. I always wondered why she had never dated again. She was such a stunning woman who also always seemed to know more than she let on.

"Okay, I let you eat in peace. I thought a full stomach would make you more forthcoming, but I guess I must take extreme measures to pull the truth out of you," she told me with her hands on her hips. "No peach cobbler until you talk."

"Mommy," I protested.

"Talk."

"That's not fair. You're playing dirty. You know peach cobbler is my favorite."

"I know, which is why I knew I could use it against you. So?"

She sat down at the table across from me and interlocked her fingers. She wasn't going to let it go. Once her antennas picked up something, she saw it all the way through.

"I caught the person I thought I really liked with someone else," I finally said.

"Oh, baby, is that all? And here, I thought you would say something crazy happened."

"The person I caught him with was a man."

"Oh . . . Well, that'll do it. I'll go get you some cobbler now. And a shot. You want some tequila?"

"Mommy," I whined again, that time with a hint of a smile.

"What? Girl, I've never been through anything like that. So, if you don't take a shot, I will."

And that she did. She poured both of us a shot of tequila and brought them back to the table. It was still morning, but it had to be happy hour somewhere. So we tossed them back, and I was happy it went down smoothly.

"All right, now, where were we? Oh yes, you were telling me how you found out that your boyfriend is gay."

"He's not my boyfriend, just someone I was dating."

"Whew, well, that's good. You won't have to explain it to anyone. Make sure you go to the clinic and get checked out. If he's doing that in secret, ain't no telling what other scandalous mess he's into."

"I will, I promise. I guess I'm still caught in the shock of it all. And it's not like I can just ignore him. I still need to attend his class."

"Wait, Nori. Were you messing with one of your professors?" she asked, disappointed.

"What's wrong with that?"

"Um, nothing except the fact that you both can get into a world of trouble—especially since you're doing so well in all your classes. They could attribute it to bribery."

"Mommy, I swear I've earned all my grades the right way. Plus, word of us seeing each other won't even make it anywhere. Especially now that he knows I know his dirty little secret."

"Good. I'm sorry you had to go through that, baby. I can tell by how distraught you looked that you must have liked him. But look at it as a silver lining. Imagine actually getting deep in a relationship and finding *that* skeleton lying in his closet."

"I think I would feel the same," I told her. "But I get what you mean. Better sooner than later."

I grew quiet again, allowing myself to enter the deepest part of my mind. I was still in the moment, so the feelings were still present. However, my unpleasant feelings toward the professor would fade. And then he too would fade from my memory. He was but a blip in my life. But there was one person that would be around much longer than that.

"Is that ailing your mind?" my all-knowing mother asked.

I again looked into her brown eyes and wondered if I should tell her what her other daughter had been up to. But how could I betray Nadi's trust? Especially with what she was already dealing with. Still, a big part of me felt that my mom should know—especially since the journal was from her lineage.

"It's—"

"Nadi!" My mom yelled out, staring at something behind me with wide eyes.

I turned in my chair and saw Nadi standing there, looking like life had just collapsed on her. She wasn't crying, but I could tell she had been. Her red, puffy eyes were a dead giveaway. She seemed surprised to see me there but also relieved. From her appearance, I assumed the confrontation with Kelz hadn't gone well.

"I . . . I came here for Mommy. But I'm . . . I'm . . ." Nadi blinked feverishly to keep her tears away.

I jumped up from my seat and wrapped my arms around her shoulders, holding her tight. She held me back, and I felt her heated tears on my neck.

"I'm glad you're here too," I said lightly.

"What's going on with you two?" Mom asked when we released each other. "First, Nori finds out her boyfriend is gay, and now you show up here looking like someone took everything you have."

"Wait, what?" Nadi asked, looking at me.

"Professor Berkley. I was kind of dating him. I saw him getting his dick sucked by a man. There. Now, you're all caught up. So, tell me what happened with Kelz."

"That was a lot to swallow, but you can catch me up later," Nadi said, plopping down in an empty seat at the table. "But Kelz and I broke up."

"Oh, honey, I'm sorry." Our mom grabbed her hand and squeezed it.

"So he admitted to double-crossing you and stealing the artifacts back?" I blurted out.

Nadi cut her eyes at me, and I realized I'd said too much. Slowly, we looked at our mother, who was staring at us with her mouth slightly agape. Her eyes went from me and then to Nadi and stayed there.

"The *what* back?" she asked.

"Mommy—"

"I *know* you don't mean what I think you mean."

"It's just . . . I . . . We . . . Help me, big mouth!" Nadi's eyes pled with me.

"What do you want *me* to say?" I asked, holding my palms up.

"Nadi and Norielle, I'm so . . . You two . . . This . . . I need more liquor."

She left us at the table and went to pour herself another shot. After she tossed it back, I watched her take a few deep breaths before turning back to us. She didn't look angry. More like disappointed when she started to speak.

"Here I thought you were working some great job at a firm, and that's how you afford all these luxuries. I should have known you were lying; you dropped out of college. It's who you know, not *what* you know, my ass! When you say 'artifacts,' I can only assume you mean treasures. Correct?"

"Yes," Nadi answered truthfully.

"And these are treasures you learned about . . . *where* exactly?"

"In . . . Giovanni's journal," Nadi answered truthfully again.

"You found them?"

"Not all of them. Nowhere near half, truthfully. But a lot of them, yes. Collectors hire me to find things. A lot of them have been in the journal. So I find them, and they buy them from me."

"And Kelz helped her," I said, ignoring the evil look Nadi was giving me. "She found out today that when they would sell an item to a buyer, he would double back and rob them to sell it again."

"Oh my. My, my, my. Nadi, *what* are you doing? And to involve other people in it is ludicrous. Especially letting them know about the journal's existence."

"Mommy, I'm sorry. It's just . . . the money—"

"Ha!" she scoffed at Nadi's poor excuse. "Trading money for things so priceless. It goes against everything I ever taught you girls. You must stop immediately."

"I'm done. You won't have to worry about it anymore. I refuse to be used."

"It's not just that. I thought the journal would be safe in your hands. I thought you would want to protect the treasures—not exploit them."

"I didn't," I spoke up in defense.

"You might as well have. You didn't stop her, and you fed off the fat of the land. You're no better than she is," our mom exclaimed. "The things that journal contains would take the most uncurious and boring minds not to want to find, but that doesn't mean you should."

"Why?" Nadi asked.

"It's not just our family's most precious family heirloom, but it's also why, even when you don't realize it, we're constantly in danger. For example, did you know my great-great-grandfather, Giovanni, secretly changed his last name?"

"Why?" It was my turn to ask.

"To keep his legacy safe. To keep his family safe. People would kill to possess something so lucrative. What you're doing is dangerous, Nadi. It won't be long until someone realizes exactly how you're locating all these lost artifacts—if they haven't already."

Chapter 13

Kelz

Being the realest in a room of people meant nothing if I wasn't the realest in the room when I was by myself. The hardest object in the world to lift was the mirror to my face, but at times, it was necessary. And the recent events in my life made it necessary. I couldn't get Nadi's face out of my head. It lingered there. The disgust and disappointed look she had would haunt me forever. I watched her love for me diminish right before my eyes when she realized I wasn't who she thought I was. Forget my ego being bruised; my heart was black and blue. I had only myself to blame for that, and it was also my fault that she wouldn't answer any of my phone calls. I couldn't say I expected her to, but still, I called and sent messages.

For weeks, I tried to reach out to my baby, but if I knew her like I thought, she was done with me. Disloyalty was something she couldn't stomach.

And if the shoe were on the other foot, I'd be the same way. The void I felt with her gone was so strong that I would do just about anything to fill it. Even give up the game. It was a thought I'd played with a few times, but it never seemed like the right time. Also, I'd always been the kind of man who spent money fast, so I had to keep the money fountain flowing. At the moment, my account was sitting nicely. A slight change in my lifestyle would keep it that way.

Since Nadi was out of the game, I was back in the streets. Zeus had Banks and me collecting for him again and watching his organization, making sure everything was running smoothly. It was familiar territory, but still not enough to keep the intrusive thoughts of doing away with it all for good anyway. However, when Zeus called me and told me he had something major on the floor, I couldn't help but think it might be the bag I needed to put the life of drugs and robbery behind me officially.

On the way to Zeus's, Banks, of course, rode shotgun with me. He was quiet, quieter than he usually was. He did not try to hide that he wasn't happy with Nadi pulling the plug on things. But it was something he would just have to get over. There was no going back to that. I played my music loudly to fill in the silence and felt the bass bumping through my seat. When we finally reached the tall gates of Zeus's estate, I turned the music down and pulled through, nodding at his workers. I parked in front of the house and made to get out, but Banks spoke and stopped me.

"Man, what's this shit about?" he asked, pointing at the tall mansion.

"We talked about this already. Zeus said he has something on the floor for us to pick up."

"I know, but what is it?"

"If I knew, don't you think I would have told you?" I asked, and he gave me a look that said I was on BS. "Bro, we're both blind right now. So you telling me you don't want to go up in here and hear the offer?"

"I guess we don't have a choice, do we? Now that your bitch done cut us off."

"Watch your mouth. That's the last time I'ma say that shit, Banks," I warned. "And you always have a choice. You can choose to get this money with me, or you can bounce. I won't even make it hard for you."

"Fuck all that. We had the perfect hustle going on, and she just ghosted us like that," Banks gruffly stated and shook his head.

"We lied to her."

"No, *you* lied to her. So *you* need to fix it. All Zeus wanna do is keep us in the streets, and you know it. We had him eating from the palms of our hands. Now, we're back to eating from his."

"Banks, get this through your head. That shit we had going is over. Nadi ain't fucking with us, and without her, we don't know the first thing about finding an artifact. So let's do what we know how to do."

"We don't need Zeus. We were doing just fine before we got roped in his shit. I say you, me, Charles, and Coney pick up where we left off before you met Nadi."

"No."

"Why not?"

"Because it's not smart. That's why, stupid. Did you forget what you did?"

"You mean what *we* did?"

"No, motherfucka. What *you* did. Your head is too hot, and a lot of times, you don't think. So if you want to go back to snatching chains and running hustlers' pockets, you do that. But me? I need the biggest bag I can get."

"Man, you just like being Zeus's bitch. All up that motherfucka's ass."

"What?" I snarled.

"You heard me, Kelz. Got Zeus thinking you're the boss over here or something."

"You jealous?"

"Never that. I just want both you *and* that nigga to know *I* ain't got no boss. I'm here for the money, and that's it."

"If that's the case, I'm sure you won't mind shutting the fuck up so we can go in here and get this bag."

I got out of the car, not caring if Banks decided to follow. However, his words had me fuming. It seemed that he forgot *I* was the one responsible for always making the plays, and *he* was the one always messing up.

I walked up the steps to the front door and then heard a car door slam shut. Shortly after, Banks appeared at my side. We didn't say another word to each other. Suddenly, in front of us, one of the tall double doors flung open, and Zeus's newest girl, Shalia, greeted us. She was looking right and wearing a robe over red lingerie.

"Goddamn," Banks said, eyeing her thirstily. "You know you need to be with a king like me, right? Your man ain't the only one with bread."

Shalia looked him up and down before giving a small laugh. Banks might have had some paper, but he was a mere penny compared to Zeus. And from the looks of it, Zeus treated his women well enough *never* to want to leave.

"Not too much, um . . . What's your name again?" she asked.

"Banks, baby girl. You need to embed *that* in your head."

"That's right, Banks. Well, you might have a couple of dollars, but ironically, I want the whole bank. I'm good where I'm at. Follow me. Zeus is in his office waiting for you."

When she turned around and started walking, I couldn't stop my eyes from lowering to her round bottom. It jiggled as she swished and made me miss watching Nadi doing the same thing as she walked away. Finally, I snapped out of it and followed her with Banks in tow.

When we reached Zeus's office, two men stood outside, ready to protect him even in his own house. Shalia took her leave once she got us where we needed to go. In the office, Zeus was sitting at his desk reviewing some paperwork. He was clean, as usual, dressed in his standard suit and tie attire. When we entered the office, he looked up from the document he was reading and smiled.

"Kelz, my boy." He stood to shake my hand.

"What's good, Zeus?" I grinned. "You in here handling business as usual?"

"You know, if I don't keep this boat floating, nobody will. Have a seat," he said, and when we sat, he turned his attention to Banks. "Long time no see, Banks."

"You know me. I just like moving in the shadows," Banks responded, not returning Zeus's smile.

"I hear you." Zeus nodded and then turned back to me. "Since you're taking a break from our other business dealings, I figured I could put you to use elsewhere. But now that I think of it, you never told me why you won't be able to procure me any more valuable items."

"After what happened to Daugherty, I think we should lie low for a while. I don't like seeing my handiwork on the news," I answered evenly, and Zeus seemed to accept the response.

"That's very disappointing, but I understand. I'll just have to enjoy the pieces that I have for now. I'm sure you're ready to hear all about the business proposition I have for you."

"You'd be right about that. I usually only show my face when money is involved."

"Then my next words should be music to your ears. You know, since I met you, your ambition has been the thing that stood out to me. You always seem to be trying to reach the next level, which could threaten a man in my position. Someone like me could feel that someone like you might gun for my crown at any time."

"So why am I still alive then?" I heard myself ask.

"Because why would you take a crown that could be inherited one day? I wasn't blessed with the ability to have children, but I have my business, and it's as much my baby as something that's flesh and blood. I'll be gone one day, and when that day comes, I want my legacy to be in capable hands."

"Ain't that what Zayle is for?"

"Zayle is somebody I trust with my life, yes. But he's as old as I am. He'll be right behind me when I go if he hasn't croaked already. Outside of him, there's nobody else I would want in my seat besides you."

"Why me? I'm sure somebody else in your camp has worked under you longer than me that you can groom."

"Ahh, and this is where the first lesson starts, my boy. Do you know why there is only one king-pin in every operation?"

I opened my mouth to answer, but when I tried to, I realized that I'd never really thought about it before. And because of that, I knew I didn't have an answer. So instead of speaking, I closed my mouth to listen.

"Because he has all the power and shooters. Fear brings that money and respect in," Banks said, and Zeus chuckled.

"You're almost there, but not quite. That kind of thinking leads the blind to try to conquer the throne. But it's also that kind of thinking that ruins an empire," Zeus told him. "That throne will tell you if you belong or not. This is about more than selling drugs and getting cash. This is politics, my boy. You must be able to be a chameleon and blend into every background, every social scene. You must be a known face and a ghost at the same time. This isn't a game about fear or respect. It's about always having pieces in the right positions. A kingpin is only as powerful as his connections. You'll lose every time if you're only focused on one part of the game, which is why not every hustler can be the kingpin because they're only focused on *being* the kingpin."

Words of wisdom. They hit me deeply. I didn't know if it was because it opened my mind to a new way of thinking or because I had never even toyed with the thought of being in Zeus's position. I made my own bubbles and rode my own waves. I never was the type to check to see if anybody else's grass was greener. I was too busy watering my own.

"I guess I'm still a little confused about why you would consider passing me such a high position. I'm not even from here."

"Your humility is telling me that I'm right about you. You know how to take care of your team and make sure that everyone is fed. Also, you know how to be a chameleon. These may seem like simple feats, but I assure you not many can do both. I obviously would need to see you in a position of power before making my final decision, so here comes my proposition."

"I'm listening," I said, leaning back in my seat.

"How would you like to control your own territory? You would push my work but be in full control of everything else. Including all the people under you."

"That sounds good, but what's the catch?"

He might have been serious, but he had laid it on thick. I wasn't born yesterday, and I knew that there was a good reason when a man held a pot of gold that heavy in front of you. And it usually wasn't just because "he saw something in you." Zeus and I connected eyes, and I could tell by how his jaw clenched slightly that I was right. There *was* a catch.

"LA needs . . . a cleansing, for lack of better terms. In my fascination with becoming rich in other ways, a few things have slipped through my fingers in my streets. One is Arnell 'Dub' Lewis. He's always been a thorn in my side, but now he's aligned with Nicolo Brasi, Lamont Crawford, and Rashad Bailey. Do you know who they are?"

"No, I don't."

"They used to work for me but broke away long ago to align with one another. Dub used to be as close to me as Zayle is. But he grew power hungry and made his own operation, taking away major keys to mine."

"Why didn't you just blow that motherfucka out of the water?" Banks asked.

"Politics, my dear boy. Politics. He has some very powerful players who are loyal to him. I could win a war with him, but not without taking many losses and putting unwanted eyes on all that I've built. And *that's* where you come in."

"I'm listening."

"You and your team have shown me that you can gain access to the rarest and most priceless items, so I know you can get close to any man. Close enough to kill him. Your faces are unknown to most, and few except my most loyal can connect you to me. I want you to eliminate all the names I just gave you."

"And take over one of their territories?" I said as all the dots connected.

"Precisely."

"Hold on. I count four territories," Banks noted. "What are your plans with the other three? I could—"

"I appreciate all the work you've done for me up until now, Banks, but I don't know much about you except that you follow Kelz's orders. If you think I'd entrust such a big part of my operation to you, save your breath. Respectfully." Zeus cut his eyes at Banks, then turned back to me. "For four wannabe kingpins, I need four funerals. What do you think about the Murder Express?"

"Murder Express, huh?" I said, rubbing my chin. "That sounds good and all, but I'm a businessman first and foremost. Four major bodies to drop, and in return, I get some territory and groomed to be king? That's not enough to seal the deal for me. So what's the price per head?"

"Spoken like a true businessman." Zeus chuckled and clasped his hands together. "Three fifty a head."

Banks whistled beside me. It was a hefty amount and proved how badly Zeus wanted the four of them gone. I pondered over the offer even though there wasn't much to think about. The pros were very lucrative, but there was one heavy con. I hadn't planned a hit without Nadi in years. She was the one who filled in all of the gaps and tiniest details. Her mind worked in a way mine just didn't. I knew it would be a long shot, but I needed her. So I had to figure out how to get her in on the deal. With her by my side, we wouldn't fail. If all went well, forget the territory. That was the kind of job I needed to step away from the game.

"We're in," I said, ignoring the burning gaze Banks was shooting my way and focused all my attention on a smiling Zeus.

"I knew I could count on you," Zeus said, reaching his hand over the desk.

"Send me all the information that I need, and we'll handle it," I said, and we shook on it.

Banks and I stood up to leave, and when we were almost out the door, Zeus cleared his throat.

"There's one tiny thing I forgot to mention," he said when I turned around. "I want this done quickly."

"How quick?"

"By the end of this month."

"That's a little over two weeks away," Banks noted with wide eyes.

"We can handle it," I assured Zeus.

"Good. You can show yourselves out."

And that we did. I left Zeus's house feeling good about the deal we'd just made. If I could slip in and out of the most guarded homes unscathed and, most times, undetected, doing what Zeus needed was a piece of cake. On the other hand, Banks seemed to have different feelings about what had happened. I could tell by the way his back was hunched that he wasn't happy. I thought he would be pleased since the job paid just as much as working with Nadi did. I walked quickly to catch up to him before he got in the car. I grabbed his shoulder and whipped him around to face me.

"Aye, what's your problem?"

"Are you out of your fucking mind?" Banks asked. "How the hell are we supposed to pull this shit off in two weeks? We don't know anything about these people."

"We've done more with much less," I reminded him. "You heard the price just like I did. So you wanted to leave that on the floor for somebody else to pick up?"

"That's not the point. And another thing. Contrary to what Zeus thinks, you're *not* my boss. You *don't* speak for me. You, me, Coney, and

Charles should have sat down and discussed this. Instead, you gave the go without consent from all of us, and I'm sure the others would think that was fucked up too."

"I don't think they would. You know why?"

"Why is that?"

"Because Coney and Charles know how to stay in their fucking place," I barked. "You keep running your mouth about not having a boss when everything we are and do is because of me. My moves, my plays, my fucking game. I would tell you to fall in line, but you've been in line. And I'm tired of you acting like you already don't know what it is. I love you like a brother, and that's the only reason I keep you by my side, but if you fuck up one more time, you're done. Now, get in the fucking car so we can go."

I got in and slammed my door. When Banks did the same, his energy had shifted again. I couldn't read it, and honestly, I didn't care to. The only thing on my mind was plotting the next move.

Chapter 14

Banks

Who the hell did Kelz think he was? It had taken every ounce of resistance I had in me not to reach over and smack the life out of him as he drove me home. But I didn't. Instead, I let him drop me off and keep it pushing. I all but slammed the front door to my condo when I walked in. If I were in a cartoon, the fumes coming from my head would be visible. Kelz was ruining everything.

Kelz, Charles, Coney, and I had come up like brothers, but I was the closest to Kelz. He was calm, and I always had the hothead, but we balanced each other. Truth be told, Kelz was a good boy when I met him. I'm the one who put him on to his first lick and his second. He wouldn't know what this life tasted like if it weren't for me.

It was an easy way to pay for our lifestyle, and it became so easy that it was second nature. After years of robbing every major hustler, we wanted a fresh hunting ground. So we all decided to move together to California. The plan had been simple back then. We only wanted to take from the rich and run it up. It had been our MO.

Thick as thieves were what Kelz and I were, no pun intended. We were equals. If he rocked, I rolled, and vice versa. One didn't make a move without the other, but that all changed when he brought Nadi into the fold. At first, he tried to make it seem like he was just using her for her information and usefulness. But a blind man could tell that he had fallen hard for her. And that's when he began to change.

"Who the fuck does this nigga think he is? Talking to me crazy and shit," I huffed as I went to my bedroom and kicked off my shoes. "He better recognize who the hell he's dealing with."

Shortly after we started working for Zeus, Kelz began acting like our group's leader. He and Zeus built a rapport. Zeus would only talk to Kelz about what needed to be done, and Kelz would relay the message. And now, I finally knew the reason for that. Zeus saw something in Kelz that he didn't see in the rest of us—that he didn't see in me. The thought of working under Kelz didn't sit right with me, especially since we had started on the same level. He didn't even try to fight for me to have my own place in Zeus's organization. After everything I had a hand in, I deserved it. But it looked like

Kelz was adopting the same god complex as the men we used to rob.

I wondered how Zeus would feel if the sides of Kelz he didn't know about came to light. Initially, the plan had been to rob Zeus, but the truth was that he was the most powerful man we'd ever encountered. His home was guarded like Fort Knox; we had never been inside long enough to case the place. Getting to his valuables would prove impossible, but his right-hand man was a different story. Zayle's god complex lied in the fact that he felt nobody would come at him because he was Zeus's right-hand man. He had significantly less security around him and his home. The night Zeus was to receive an award for all the good things he'd done for his community, Kelz and I decided to make our move.

"Let's get in and out," Kelz whispered beside me. *"Stay low to the ground. There might be more eyes on this crib than we know. Use the shadows."*

From under my mask, I nodded at him and ignored the twinge of annoyance from him telling me what to do. Instead, I adjusted the bag I carried and focused on the task at hand. We crouched down low as we approached a vehicle parked in the driveway of a quaint two-story home. The house belonged to the one and only Zayle

Heckord, underboss of LA's kingpin. I could feel the excitement pouring from my head to my toes, thinking about the crazy lick my boy and I were about to hit. It was something to sweeten the taste of my end game.

Zayle and his entourage were out for the evening, leaving the home empty and ready for the taking. The only thing in the way was the two men watching the house. I wanted with everything in me to put bullets in their heads, but Kelz was against killing unless the job called for it.

So instead, we crept to the back of the house, using Zayle's neatly manicured bushes as cover. Zayle had cameras all around the perimeter of the place, but Kelz had already jammed the signal on them and the security system, which meant we had to work fast before someone was sent in to check on them.

Kelz went to work on the back door of the house, but I grew impatient. Using a rock I found lying in the backyard, I hit the glass window, making a hole big enough for my hand to reach through and unlock the door. I couldn't see Kelz's face under his mask, but the repulsive look in his eyes told no lies.

"You were taking too long," I said, sliding the door open. "After you."

He shook his head and went through the door after pulling out his pistol. I checked the sur-

roundings to make sure nobody was watching and followed him. He went one way, and I went the other as we quickly checked the lower level of the house. As I suspected, no one was inside. We steered clear of the windows toward the front of the house and went upstairs to where the rooms were.

"Where you think he keeps the safe? The bedroom, huh?" I asked and started toward the master bedroom.

"Nah. A man like Zayle wouldn't keep something like that in his bedroom. That's where he brings his women, and that motherfucka doesn't trust anybody. So the safe will be somewhere he can lock and somewhere he's always awake in. His office. Let's check there."

"You go check there. I'ma hit the bedroom," I told him defiantly, and we split up.

Covering more ground was the smartest thing to do. I pulled out a small flashlight when I reached the master bedroom to navigate the darkness. I swept it across the dresser and spotted a square box wrapped in metallic blue paper with a bow. I removed the top and stared at a gold and black diamond-encrusted Richard Mille watch.

"Goddamn," I whispered at the find.

After putting it in my pocket, I searched for the bigger lick. I checked behind every photo on the wall and came up empty-handed. There was *nothing under the bed or hidden in the closet, either. The last place I checked was his dresser. Besides some kinky man panties, I didn't find anything there. Kelz had been right. I was about to find him so he could rub it in my face, but I heard him on his way to me. Except . . . The more I listened, I realized that it wasn't Kelz.*

"Zayle, I'm grabbing the gift right now. I'll be back at the event in a second," the voice said cheerfully, talking on the phone. "Yeah, man, you know Zeus is going to shit bricks when he sees how you came with this one. All right. Love you, big bro."

When the man entered the room, I'd already screwed the silencer on my gun. It was Zaire, Zayle's younger brother. I'd only seen him a few times in passing, so I was sure he wouldn't be able to recognize my voice. There weren't many places to hide, so I didn't even try to. I could have slid under the bed or entered the closet, but he would have heard the movement. Either way, when he stepped into the bedroom, he saw a tall man wearing a mask and holding a gun. He froze in his steps and blinked, almost as if he were trying to make sure he was seeing correctly.

"Hmm," he said in an amused voice. "Now it makes sense why the alarm was acting funny. Who the hell are you, and what are you doing in my brother's house?"

"Mask plus gun. Obviously, I'm robbing the place," I said, pointing the gun at him.

"Well, that's stupid. Do you know who my brother is?"

"Who doesn't know who Zayle is?"

"Then you must know this is the craziest thing anyone could do, especially when he finds out. My brother doesn't take too kindly to peoples going through his shit."

"Who says he's going to find out?" I said with a small laugh.

"He's going to kill you. You know that, right? You're crazy."

"What's crazy is I had no idea that such a treasure would fall into my lap tonight," I said, smirking under my mask. "See, there's nothing like breaking your prey down from the inside, making them squirm because they don't know what or who is making them tick. To my partner, this is a simple lick on an asshole. But to me, this is the means to the end of an empire. See, when a man is nervous, he lets his weak spots show without realizing it, and this violation of Zayle's home will reveal them all. And once he's gone, it's on to the bigger fish. Zeus."

"It's not going to work. Zeus is untouchable."

"Except, I've already touched him," I said, feeling the wide smile come to my lips. "He doesn't even know it. All the pieces are falling into place, and his days are numbered."

"*You can try, but like I said, it won't work.*" *Zaire shrugged.*

"*Before this moment, I knew it was a fifty-fifty chance, but now, I know it will work. I was going to play with Zayle's head by violating his home. But now, I'm going to do something so much better.*"

"*And what's that? Hold me hostage?*"

"*No,*" *I chuckled.* "*This ain't a movie, mother-fucka. I will break his heart by taking his baby brother's soul.*"

His hand moved to the gun on his waist, but I had the advantage. Mine was already pointed at his head. One quick pull on the trigger sent a bullet crashing into his head, snapping it back. As his body collapsed to the floor, I saw a stunned Kelz standing behind him, staring in horror.

"*Banks, what the fuck did you just do?*"

I felt a tingle of satisfaction as the memory of Zaire's dead body faded from my mind. That night, Kelz had come just as I shot Zaire, so he hadn't heard the earlier conversation, which was good. I had banked on Zayle becoming Zeus's weakest link after the death of his brother, which he did. But what I didn't bank on was Zeus's ability to attempt to replace him so quickly. It didn't take a rocket scientist to see how he was moving Kelz into position. But before that happened, I would ensure they were all six feet deep in caskets.

Knock, knock.

Not surprised to hear someone knocking at my door, I went to open it. I looked down at the beautiful face and body attached to it. Any other time I would be happy to see my shawty standing there, but right then, I was annoyed.

"You're late," I said and let Shalia inside.

"Yeah, well, after you and Kelz left, it was hard to sneak away," she said, rolling her eyes.

She set her Chanel bag on the dining room table and plopped down in one of the chairs. The bag was new, and so were the matching heels. I knew Zeus had bought them for her. Although it was my idea to put her on him and play the part of one of his women, I wondered if she was getting too comfortable in his camp.

"Nice shoes," I commented, and she rolled her eyes again.

"Please don't start this shit. You're the one who put me on Zeus. I didn't think this shit would take so long. But while I'm doing my job, I don't see nothing wrong with cashing in on the gifts."

"Yeah, yeah. Whatever."

I'd met Shalia at Black Diamonds, a local strip club, shortly after I'd moved to California. She'd been dancing on the pole with purple strobe lights bouncing off her round ass. I was enticed, and what was supposed to be a one-night stand turned into much more than that. She was a hustler like me and had been on her own since she was 14. Initially, I could admit that I exploited her need to be loved and cared for. What I didn't know was that I had those same needs. Ultimately, I fell for her mind and the fact that she was the only one who accepted me for me—flaws and all. She didn't try to fix me and wasn't afraid of my anger. In fact, in every sense, she matched me.

I hadn't told anyone about the two of us being involved, but she was on the same takeover vibe I was. And she was also thorough. It was a Bonnie-and-Clyde vibe with us, and as much as I didn't want to admit it sometimes, I loved her. And she loved me too. So much that she would do anything for me. She was the only one who knew about my plans to get Zeus out of the way and take over his operation. She was also more than happy to assist with it. I'd shared everything with Kelz, and now I wanted to be something individual, something I had never got to be before—the king.

"What's the word?" I asked.

"Nothing much. Zeus is mad that Kelz doesn't want to find rare artifacts for his collection any-more, but he isn't showing that. Instead, he's now obsessed with finding some journal. I don't know, but if you ask me, all that shit is weird."

"Nah, you just don't know anything about the finer things in life for real."

"Um, hello? Chanel bag," she said, rolling her neck and pointing at the purse.

"That's half a penny in comparison, shawty. Anyway, tell me more about this journal."

"I don't know. Something called Giovanni's journal. It's supposed to have damn near an endless number of rare artifacts in it. When I say he's obsessed, he's obsessed. It was probably the next thing on his list he wanted y'all to find."

"Mm, never heard of it."

"I bet. When is all this going to be over, baby? I'm tired of fucking that old-ass man. I don't care how much money he has. I'd rather be here with you."

"Shit done changed. I noticed he upped security."

"That's your fault. You're the one who killed Zaire. That's fucking with all their heads that they don't know who did it."

"It's making him damn near untouchable. Not only that, but he's also putting Kelz in a position to run his own territory after this next little job."

"What? And not you? You've put in just as much work as Kelz."

"Exactly. But it won't matter. Kelz is going to be dead right along with the rest of them."

"But . . . Isn't that your brother?"

Her words lingered, and I remembered how Kelz had spoken to me. I also recalled how he and Zeus had treated me like a little boy in the meeting. My chest grew tight, and I shook my head.

"Not anymore. It's eat or be eaten."

"Well, what are you going to do?" she asked, and I smiled, looking at the Richard Mille watch on my wrist.

"I got something cooking up; you'll see. But the less you know right now, the better," I said, standing before her and unzipping my pants. "All I want you to do right now is suck this dick how I like it."

Whipping my joystick out, I all but shoved it down Shalia's throat. Her hands gripped my sides, and she took control. I watched her make my shaft disappear and reappear, each time making it wetter than before. The warmth of her tongue swirling around the tip made me feel like I was floating. I couldn't believe I would share those skills with another man. Images of Zeus taking her to pound town suddenly plagued my mind. I knew her being there was my idea, but suddenly, she felt dirty to me. I pushed her off me and zipped up my pants.

"Baby, what's wrong?" she asked, bewildered.

"Nothing," I said gruffly. "Go on and head back to Zeus's crib. Suck his dick or somethin'. I have some shit to handle here."

"Oh, so *that's* what this is about, huh? So you're jealous," she said, jumping up. "Don't forget that this was *your* plan. I'm just trying to help you out."

"Ever thought you're doing your job a little too well?" I asked and waved a hand toward the door. "Go before he gets suspicious. I'll call you."

"Whatever," she huffed.

I could tell that I'd hurt her feelings by denying her. She didn't even look at me on her way out. I followed behind her and opened the door, but before she stepped out, I grabbed her arm.

"This shit will all be over soon, okay?"

"But will it really? After I do my job, will you even want to touch me? Will we be the same?" she asked and pulled away from me.

"You know it's me and you. I'm just fucked up right now," I said and kissed her forehead. "Make sure you let me know all that old motherfucka's moves, okay?"

"Yeah, okay."

I let her leave with my lie hanging in the air. I didn't know if things would go back to how they were when I met her. Especially with the images of her and Zeus in my head. But in the meantime, I needed to ensure she did her job right. So I made a mental note to send her a sweet text message in the morning to get back in her good graces. In the meantime, there was somebody that I needed to set up a meeting with.

Walking back to my bedroom, I pulled out my phone and dialed a number. It was my third attempt to make contact since my call was ignored the first two times. My eyes went to the watch on my wrist as I listened to the phone ring. On the fourth ring, someone finally answered.

"Who the fuck is this, and how did you get this number?" an angry voice said on the other end.

"Zayle, it's me, Banks. We should talk. I know who killed your brother."

Chapter 15

Nadi

Maneuvering around with a broken heart? Something I would never recommend. I could remember how heavy I felt when my dad died. I didn't think I'd ever feel anything near to it again. But there I was, sulking in my bedroom under the covers and looking at the same four walls. The only thing I'd found the strength to do was shower and then climb right back into bed.

With Kelz, there was never an escape plan. Once we got together, I never even toyed with the thought of experiencing a day without him again. I loved him. Even in my anger, I loved him. And that was why I was so sad.

I stopped thinking about why he did what he did. Money messed with people's heads in the worst ways. It wasn't an excuse; it was the truth. Money was more important to him than me, and it was something I forced myself to swallow early on.

I was allowing myself to feel what I needed to feel so I could move on with my life.

I didn't know what I wanted to do. I could go back to school or start a business, but I would need to put more thought into it. What I really needed to do was take a trip to clear my mind. One filled with serene views and feels. I could picture myself being gone for a month or two before returning home. I grabbed my phone from the nightstand to check my account balance. I hadn't looked at it since right before Kelz and I did our drop-off to Daugherty. I expected to see three commas due to the last jobs I partook in, but the number looking back at me made me suddenly sit up in anguish.

"Two hundred thousand dollars?" I said out loud, looking down at my phone.

I checked my incoming transfers because the account should have had well over a million dollars. There were no transfers or recent deposit transactions. My blood began to boil. I could have attributed things to Kelz just forgetting to send my money, but no. He had never failed to do it before. I couldn't believe him. First, he crossed me, only to turn around and do it again by stealing from me. I jumped up from my bed. It would have been easy to make a phone call, but something like that needed to be discussed face-to-face. I hurried to throw some clothes on and brush my hair into a ponytail. After grabbing my keys, I was about to leave, but my bedroom door swung open. Nori poked her head in and looked surprised to see me out of bed.

"Where you going?" she asked, seeing the keys in my hand.

"Just out to get some fresh air," I answered.

"Oh yeah? Let me throw on my shoes. I'll come with."

"No, I want to go alone."

I brushed past her and walked to the front door with her on my heels. She watched closely as I grabbed my purse and sunglasses from the island. I wanted to leave before she started asking me a million and one questions, but I might have been too late for that.

"You're going to see Kelz, aren't you?" she asked.

"It's not what you think," I sighed.

"Sis." She grabbed my hand and made me face her. "I know it's hard letting go, but you're doing the right thing. You deserve better than Kelz. After all he's done to you, I thought you would know that by now."

"I *said* it's not what you think."

"Then what is it?"

"He owes me money. I'm going to get it. Simple."

"Are you sure that's it?" Nori gave me a doubtful look.

"Yes."

"Nadi—"

"Nori, drop it, please. You don't see me around here giving you unwarranted advice about sleeping with your college professor. Or judging the fact that he's bisexual."

"As quiet as you've been these past weeks, I would have gladly talked about it with you," she shot back. "Not all of us are shut off from the world."

"Whatever."

I left the condo before she could sneak out another word of advice. I didn't ask for it. She didn't see me playing Dr. Phil every chance I could. It was annoying. Once I got in my McLaren, I turned my phone on silent, knowing there was a good chance of Nori blowing it up with messages.

The drive to Kelz's place had never seemed so long. It had been the longest we'd ever gone without seeing each other. I wondered how he would react to seeing me standing outside his door. And if he didn't give me what I came for, I wondered how he would respond to my fist in his face.

When I arrived, I saw a red convertible parked in his guest parking spot. I'd never seen the car before, but my heart began beating fast. Did he have company? Was it a woman? I almost didn't get out of the car, fearful of what I might do if he had a woman inside his place. If we were over for real, I shouldn't have cared, right? Right . . . but I did. Kind of. I sat up straight and told myself I was there for one reason and one reason only. That was to get my money and leave. If he had romantic company, I would act like I didn't care and tough it out like I'd been doing.

I got out of my car and marched inside the condo. By the time I got on the elevator, I finally got control of my breathing. Looking into the mirrored walls, I wished I hadn't left home so hastily. I was wearing plain jeans and a T-shirt. That didn't give off enough bad bitch energy for me. I wanted to look like I was living it up without Kelz. I wanted him to think I was happy.

When I got off the elevator, I put on some lip gloss on the way to Kelz's door, and when I got there, I forced away any sadness I felt at the moment.

Knock, knock.

Wait. I hadn't meant to knock on the door yet. Oh my goodness, I looked a mess. I wanted to run back to the elevator. What if he was screwing the woman parked in my spot, and I was interrupting them? What if—

"Nadi?"

I had just turned to walk away when the door opened. Kelz was standing there shirtless and giving me a confused look. I cleared my throat and faced him again, putting on my best no-nonsense face.

"Kelz."

"What are you doing here, Nadi?" he asked.

I couldn't help but feel like he was blocking the doorway, so I couldn't see inside. Also, I didn't know him not to be fully dressed in the middle of the afternoon. His hair was slightly messy, and he didn't seem happy at all to see me.

"You know why I'm here," I said finally. "Aren't you going to invite me inside?"

"Um," he said and hesitantly looked over his shoulder. "Okay. Yeah, come in."

He moved out of the way, and I peered inside. I didn't see anyone or hear anything. I pursed my lips at him.

"Mmm," I said and stepped into his place. "You have company?"

"Nah. It's just me here," he told me and locked the door. "You know I don't like people to know where I lay my head for real."

"You sure? There's a red convertible parked in your guest parking."

"I don't know who they are. I've already reported it to the management. So far, they haven't said anything to whoever drives the car."

"Right."

"You're welcome to check, though," he said, sensing my reluctance to believe him.

"That won't be necessary. You're a single man now, so you can do whatever you want."

"Is that how you really feel?"

His eyes bore into mine like they did when we would make love. They made a familiar connection to my soul and told me he loved me more than anything. I had to blink a few times to sever that connection. I wouldn't let him get me again with his love tunes. *They are not real*, I told myself. *They are all fake.*

"I'm not here to talk about that," I said, pulling up my account information and showing him. "I'm here because you never sent me what's owed me from the last job."

To my surprise, he didn't seem shocked. I expected a little shock because a big piece of me wanted to believe that he wouldn't do something like that on purpose. After all, he was a businessman at the end of the day.

"I thought you'd come by sooner."

There was a longing in his gaze that I recognized, and I felt my entire body begin to tingle. Every fiber of my being wanted to reach out to him and appease that longing, but I kept my feet planted.

"What do you mean 'sooner'?"

"You weren't talking to me. I thought . . . I figured . . ."

"That you'd hold my money and make me come to you?" I scoffed and shook my head. "I should've known you'd do something so shady. Send me my money, Kelz."

"Not until you let me explain."

"Explain what? More details of how you crossed me?"

"That wasn't my intention, Nadi. I'm a hustler. But I fell in love with you."

I scoffed again. He had some nerve. Right to my face telling me that he had used me. It was a tough pill to swallow because, in my memory, everything seemed so real. It felt so real too.

"Kelz, please, my money."

"Listen," he shouted, gently gripping my arms, forcing me to look at him. "I fucked up, baby. I fucked up. I was greedy, but in my mind, I was making the best decision at the time. It was selfish, I know. But what's mine will always be yours."

"Why'd you lie to me about what you were doing?"

"Your hands might be a little dirty, but mine are filthy. You wouldn't have approved of what I was doing."

"You still should have told me and given me a choice."

"I know that now. Look at me and tell me you don't love me anymore."

"I don't love you anymore, Kelz." I looked away.

"That must be why you're tripping at the thought of somebody else being in here, huh?" he said knowingly.

"I don't care who you have up in here."

"Is that right?" he asked, raising his warm hand to the nape of my neck. "Then why is your heart pounding?"

He was right. I felt it too. He was too close to me. I could smell the citrusy scent of his favorite body wash on him. And again his eyes . . . They started communicating with my soul again. Where my face didn't react, my heart did. If I didn't do something fast, I would be under his spell again.

"Move." I shoved him away from me. "Just send me what I'm owed."

The smirk on his face irritated me. Kelz knew the effect he was having on me. He was probably trying to get on my nerves on purpose. He left me in the front of his home and went to his bedroom. When he returned, he had a black duffle bag and dropped it at my feet.

"That's fifty thousand cash," he told me.

"Fifty thousand isn't even close to half of what I'm owed." I looked at him like he was crazy. "What the hell kind of game are you playing, Kelz? You think I won't go to war about my money?"

"Chill, baby. Damn. I thought Banks was the one with some screws loose. Daugherty transferred the money into one of my offshore accounts. When he died, the Feds started sniffing around like crazy, so I transferred it again to be safe."

"And you couldn't tell me that?"

"It's hard to tell someone anything when they aren't answering your calls," he said, and I rolled my eyes. "We can get it after I tie up a job here."

His words weren't received well. Unzipping the duffle bag, I saw nothing but stacks of money looking up at me. I sighed in defeat because what more could I do? I didn't want to wait any longer than I had. And it wasn't my fault the Feds were sniffing around. I wanted to punch him badly. So I did. Right in the chest.

"What was that for?" he asked, holding up his arms to defend a potential second attack.

"For getting us in this mess," I snapped.

"I guess I deserve that, but if you let me, I want to make it up to you."

"I'm not trying to be with a man I can't trust."

"I understand, but I'ma earn that back. In the meantime, I really want you in on this job."

Was he trying to reel me back into something I clearly said I was done with? I couldn't believe his nerve. So I hit him again.

"I told you I was out. I won't ever—"

"It's not that kind of job, Nadi," he interrupted me, rubbing the sore spot on his arm my fist had just hit. "Zeus wants me to do something for him. He wants my team to take out his competition."

"So you're a hit man now?"

"It's a job with a lucrative payout. But I must admit, I'm uncomfortable doing it without my right hand."

He crossed his arms and leaned on the wall behind him. I hated how attracted I was to him. I wished he would wear a shirt so I wouldn't be so distracted by his muscular build. It was becoming harder and harder not to look at the tattoos across his chest or six-pack. The way he was eyeing me, he was waiting for me to say something.

"What, Banks won't be there?" I finally found my voice.

"Yeah, he'll be there, but that's not what I'm talking about. I want you there, Nadi. No, I *need* you there. Nobody can lay down a plan like you. Banks shoots first and asks questions later, and we're going after some real heavy hitters this time. We can't afford to fuck up. So I need you on this. Plus, you already know I will cut you a big slice of the pie."

"You know . . . You have some nerve to ask something like this of me," I said and took a deep breath. I pondered over his offer even though I wanted to hit him with a big fat no. However, if we weren't acquiring items to sell anymore, having another stream of income for the moment wouldn't hurt. But I just didn't trust Kelz. He'd lied to me—for so long at that. So it was hard to say yes. "How big is the pie?"

"Three fifty a head. Four heads."

"Whew," I whistled when I heard the amount. "Zeus must really want them dead. Who are the targets?"

"Dub, Nicolo Brasi, Lamont Crawford, and Rashad Bailey."

None of their names rang a bell with me. I was only familiar with Zeus because, growing up, my mother didn't have anything nice to say about him. They must have been threats if Zeus wanted them knocked off that badly. I could only assume they would be as heavily guarded as him, which led me to wonder how four hired hands could get the job done. It also made me wonder if there was another incentive besides money.

"What aren't you telling me?" I asked.

He looked at the ground and rubbed his hands together. "Zeus wants me to take over one of their territories."

"Is that something you want to do?"

Kelz looked back at me, and his shoulders went up and fell back down.

"I don't know. The time we've spent apart got me thinking about what's important and what's not. I'm thinking about getting out of the game for good. Take some of the money I have saved and go legit. Start a few businesses. But honestly, none of that shit is worth it if you aren't with me. I love you, Nadi. Even if you don't believe me when I say those words, I love you. I'll give it all up if I can have you forever."

His words matched the sincerity written all over his face. A knot suddenly formed in my throat, and

I blinked away the tears threatening to come to my eyes. It would take more than words to get him on my good side again, but for the moment, they were enough.

"Let's get this job done first. We can iron out the kinks with us later," I told him.

He was about to open his mouth to say something else, but someone knocked on the door behind me. He held up a finger to me and went to check who it was. Seconds later, he opened it and in strolled Banks. He had a smile on his face . . . until he saw me, and it faded quickly. He looked from me and then to Kelz before shaking his head. He put his hands in the pockets of his gray joggers and sat down on one of the living room couches. It had never been a secret that we weren't fond of each other.

"I'm going to head out. I'll unblock you so you can let me know the moves." Then I put up two fingers and left with the duffle bag of money in tow. I didn't like Banks at all, but I was happy that he showed up when he did. I might have messed around and given Kelz some pussy.

Chapter 16

Kelz

I locked the door when Nadi left, even though I wanted her to stay. The entire time she'd been standing in front of me, I fought the urge not to sweep her in my arms and whisper sweet nothings in her ear. I loved when she dressed down, and her natural beauty shone through. It made me yearn for her touch even more. I wanted to make love to her and let my body tell her everything my mouth couldn't find words for, but I kept my urges in check mainly because I didn't want her to hit me again. For a woman, she was tough, and she hit hard. I wouldn't be surprised if a bruise formed on my arm.

I left Banks in the living room to go put on a shirt. When I returned from my bedroom, he still sat where I left him. He stared intently at his phone while his thumbs rapidly tapped the screen. He didn't even notice me come back into the room. I stared at him humorously because I knew the only thing that would make a man beat up his phone like that was a woman. Finally, I sat down in my recliner and waited for him to handle what he needed to handle.

"Man, bitches be trippin', boy," he groaned and put his phone in his pocket.

"You good?" I asked.

"I should be askin' you that same question. What was Nadi doin' here?"

"Just grabbing something I owed her."

"Oh, okay. I hope the moves she was talkin' about ain't what I think she's talkin' about."

Banks leaned into the couch. I could cut the tension in the room with a knife, but I figured I might as well let him know what was up. Nadi being a part of the crew made us better, and that was something he would just have to deal with.

"I told her about the job. She's in."

The room grew quiet. I expected Banks to put up some sort of fight. To say something about how she left us high and dry or how I was thirsty for her. But to my surprise, he did none of those things. Instead, he just nodded his head in acceptance.

"That's cool. You know I don't like her, but it's a fact that we all work better together. You ready to go scope out these folks?"

Nadi showing up unexpectedly had thrown me off so much that I almost forgot why I invited

Banks over in the first place. For us to take out our targets, we had to get familiar with how they moved. And since we were on a time crunch, we had to get to it. I nodded my head and stood to my feet. I was ready to go after putting on my shoes and tucking my pistol into my waist.

"They say Lamont and Rashad like to kick it at the Black Diamonds on Friday afternoons. And would you look at that? It's Friday afternoon. I figured we'd start there first."

"Cool. But, aye, let me use the bathroom real quick before we leave," Banks said and left me in the living room.

He wasn't gone long, and when he returned, he smiled and rubbed his hands. "A'ight, let's go get 'em."

It wasn't hard to blend in inside a club like the Black Diamonds. Every eye was on the naked women walking freely around the place. It wasn't even two o'clock, and it was packed. As a gentleman's club, it had everything men loved—liquor, food, and fine-ass women. Those were the key ingredients to making a man empty out his bank account if he wasn't careful. I'd only been there a few times with Banks when I first came to the city. But after I got with Nadi, I gave up that sort of thing. She was the only woman who could get my dick hard.

The women on stage were doing what they were paid to do, shake what their mothers gave them. Even Banks was in the middle of getting a lap dance from a chocolate goddess with perky breasts. Her body looked like it had been perfectly sculpted and glistened under the strobe lights. She bent over as far as she could and spread her cheeks wide, giving him a view of her shaved kitty. Banks threw a handful of ones on her when she started popping to the loud music. Shawty was thick; there was no denying that. And the way she had Banks going, he was about to forget why we were there.

"Aye, baby girl, let me holler at my mans," I said dismissively.

"But I'm not done with my dance yet," she pouted, still throwing that thing in a circle.

"You are now," I said and handed her $200.

"Hmm," she said through pursed lips.

She took the money in my hand and the money Banks had thrown at her before walking away to her next customer. My eyes followed her until she moved out of sight, but I kept staring straight ahead. It seemed that it was our lucky day. On the far side of the club were the two people we were there to see. Lamont Crawford and Rashad Bailey sat in a VIP section with bodyguards around them. The two men were around Zeus's age. Lamont was skinny with a bald head, while Rashad was more muscular and rocked a curly comb back. Both wore the same attire, suits and wedding rings. But that wasn't stopping them from touching and rubbing on any woman that walked by. They were having just as much fun as Banks had. The women dancing for them were going crazy with it. I could only assume it was because they knew the two men had no problem throwing them cash.

"Man, why didn't you let her finish the dance? She was throwin' that big motherfucka back on me," Banks whined.

"Because that's not what we're here for," I said, leaning back into the red velvet chair I sat on.

"I don't see Lamont or Rashad anywhere. So you might as well let me have some fun."

"Having fun is exactly why you didn't notice both people you just named sitting over there in VIP."

I nodded, and Banks looked over in the direction I motioned to. As he started watching our marks, I was watching him. He had been acting differently since we were at my place. First, he was not annoyed that I'd brought Nadi back into the fold. And second, not spotting Lamont and Rashad before me. Banks was usually the bloodthirsty one ready to make a move. However, right then, I wouldn't say he didn't care, but it was something.

"So what you wanna do? Follow them when they leave?" Banks asked, turning back to face me. "We probably won't get another opportunity like this to do it."

"Nah, we probably won't get another opportunity like this to kill them," I said to his shock.

"You wanna blow their heads back right now? That's risky as hell. I thought we were just scopin' out shit."

"You're the king of risk. So you should like this plan. Two birds, one stone. This is the chance of a lifetime," I stated and pointed inconspicuously at the men surrounding Rashad and Lamont. "Look there. They come here so much, they're lax on their security inside. I'm sure the rest are outside waiting."

"So what? You wanna go to war with all of them?"

"No. We make sure they never make it outside."

I stopped talking and pulled out a small bag of Special K, or ketamine. I'd already taken the liberty of crushing the pills. I learned of the drug when I was in high school. The athletes used it to loosen up girls to get in their panties. Banks and I found another use for it, though. See, the drug came in handy when we were hitting safes. Say someone wasn't being cooperative, the Special K loosened them up just enough to give us whatever information we wanted to know before we did away with them.

"What you about to do with that?" he asked, but by then, the chocolate dancer that had just left our section was walking back our way.

"Excuse me," I said, getting her attention.

She had been on her way to another patron a little ways away, but she changed course when I flashed her a thick wad of cash. As soon as she got to me, she started dancing, but I stopped her and pulled her beside me.

"What's your name, sweetheart?" I asked, turning on my charm.

"Black Cat. Cat for short."

"Well, Cat, you don't even have to do all that to get this money, shawty," I said.

"Then what you want me to do to get it? Talk to you?"

"Nah, you don't get that kind of paper working your mouth unless you're doing it on this dick," Banks told her.

"Well, you'll want Sweet Pea for that because I don't do all that. So let me go get her."

Cat made to get up, but I stopped her again. I didn't know what type of time Banks was on. I shot him a look telling him to let me do the talking.

"What you know about those two gentlemen over there?" I asked and motioned in Rashad and Lamont's direction.

"Y'all must be new here or something. That's Rashad and Lamont, two of the biggest hustlers in LA. You would think they had some coke to move, but they come in here all the time with their thirsty asses. They have paper, though. The kind that makes a man feel like he can do whatever he wants to a woman. Last week, Rashad—"

She stopped talking and looked away from me as if she'd said too much. From the disgusted look on her face, I could tell that whatever was on the tip of her tongue wasn't good. The closer I looked at her, though, I could see that the look wasn't disgust at all. It was shame.

"Rashad what?" I urged her to continue.

"Look, I know you motherfuckas come in here and look down on women like me. We dance on men with our asses and pussy out for a living. Hell, I'm sitting here talking to you naked right now. When men get handy and *do* things to us that we don't want, everybody turns a blind eye. It just comes with the business, you know?" Cat shook her head. "But fuck that. My job doesn't give anyone the right to have their way with me as they please. Or to fuck me when he wants to."

"Unless he's payin', right?" Banks said coldly.

"See?" Cat shook her head again. "Nobody gives a fuck if I don't consent. I'm just a ho to y'all."

"Shut the fuck up, Banks," I told him forcefully, and I meant it. He turned his nose up, but he didn't say anything else, and I turned back to Cat. "Excuse him. He's just a little uptight, that's all."

"I know the type," she said, looking at Banks. "The type that needs to bust a nut but just can't. You look familiar."

"We used to come here awhile back," I said, taking the conversation back to what she was talking about. "The person who has their way with you, it's Rashad?"

Cat nodded before giving a slight chuckle.

"I'm over here pouring my heart out to you like you give a fuck. Do you want a dance or not? If not, I really need to move around. I have bills."

"Nah, I don't want a dance. But I want you to do something else, though. Something that will be beneficial to both of us. If you do, I have five bands in my pockets with your name on them."

At the mention of the amount of money, Cat sat up in her seat. She eyed me curiously momentarily as if to see if I was lying. To ease her concern, I pulled more money out of my other pocket to show her.

"Fine," she finally said. "What do you need me to do?"

Cat stumbled into the men's restroom an hour later, but she wasn't alone. And I didn't mean because Banks and I secretly hid in two stalls. She had both Rashad and Lamont with her. I watched them from the small opening in the closed stall door. Their movements were that of someone who had too much to drink. However, their loopy laughter told me that the Special K I had Cat sneak into their drinks had kicked in. Two of their guards tried to come in the bathroom too, but Lamont ordered them away.

"Go out there and get your own pussy," he shouted. "Enjoy yourselves. You're always up our asses. Go stick your dicks in one of these hoes' asses."

"Boss, I—"

"Get the fuck out of here," Rashad said and made like he was about to grab his gun.

The security looked at each other before shrugging and leaving. My hand rested on my own pistol. If they were good security guards, they would have checked the stalls before they left. That was the good thing about pussy being everywhere in the building. They were only too happy to get back to it.

When they were gone, I continued watching the scene unfold. Rashad was more than a little rough with Cat as he groped her, but she let it happen with a smile.

"You like that, don't you, daddy?"

"You know I do," Rashad slurred and smacked her bottom. "Lamont, this bitch has the wettest pussy in this place."

"I'll judge that," Lamont said, grabbing Cat by the jaw. "You're going to be a good girl and take two dicks?"

"Of course, baby," Cat said seductively, sliding her hand to his crotch. "Ooh, it's big. I can't wait to feel it in my ass."

"Fuck, you're turning me on," Lamont said and scooped her up into the air.

He sucked her dark nipples while Rashad moved the amenities out of the way on the bathroom table so he could lay her down. When her legs were spread eagle, Rashad positioned himself between them while Lamont focused on getting some head. They both unzipped their pants and as soon as they dropped them to their ankles, Banks and I quickly exited our stalls. When Cat saw us with our guns drawn, she got up and ran out of the bathroom, leaving Rashad and Lamont standing there with their dicks out. Unfortunately, the moment the men saw our silencers was a moment too late.

Pffit! Pfft! Pfft! Pfft!

Each got a bullet to the head and the chest before they dropped dead to the ground. Their blood began to spill on the tiled floor, letting us know it was time to go. Banks slowly opened the door a crack and peeked outside. When he saw that the coast was clear, he opened it, and we rushed out. Instead of returning to the main floor, we ran down the hallway toward the back door. On the way, we passed the club's security room, where Cat was seducing three of the club's workers and keeping their eyes off the cameras. However, it was kind of hard to ignore the two big men standing in the doorway with guns.

"Shit!" one of them shouted, fumbling his hand at his hip.

Banks and I wasted no time laying them out too. While Banks checked to make sure they were dead, I went on ahead and erased all of the footage from that day. I also went in and deleted any backups and turned off the cameras. Once I finished, I turned to Cat.

"You did good."

"I know I did. Now, where's my money?" she asked with her hand out.

I grinned at her. It was nothing but respect for anyone who was about their paper. I reached into my pockets to get her payment.

"It's right he—"

Pfft!

Cat's head snapped to the side as Banks's bullet entered it. Her eyes were still open when she fell to the ground. I was completely caught off guard, so much so that I didn't even wipe off her blood splattered on my face. My eyes went from her dead body to Banks's coldhearted expression.

"She saw our faces. She had to go," he said in a tone that matched his demeanor. "Let's get out of here."

There was nothing I could do. I looked back down at Cat one last time before I ran out of the room. Nobody saw us exit from the back door. We ran to where I parked my car. I was breathing heavily but didn't catch my breath until I sped away from the club. When I did, I pulled out my phone and called Zeus.

"Hello?"

"Two down, two to go," I said before hanging up the phone.

Chapter 17

Zeus

The news of Rashad's and Lamont's deaths spread like wildfire. It had happened so swiftly that no one knew what to think. That, coupled with the fact that the video surveillance in the strip club where their bodies were found had been completely wiped, baffled people. Nobody in the establishment at the time saw anyone suspicious. They were too busy enjoying the amenities they'd come for. Both Rashad's and Lamont's camps thought it was an inside job at the club. But even if they figured out it wasn't, the trail wouldn't lead back to me.

Kelz once again impressed me with his precision and ability to be a ghost. He'd knocked off not one but two of his hits in a single move. He was a step closer to earning his promotion. The most powerful leader needed strong pieces on his chessboard, and Kelz would make a fine addition to mine.

Sitting in my office chair, I welcomed the burning sensation as I took a drag from the cigar between my fingers. I let the smoke sit in my lungs for a second before I blew it to the ceiling. The rich, masculine aroma filled the air, and I found myself smiling. At that moment, Rashad's and Lamont's camps were scrambling to figure out their next move, not knowing that I was coming to make it for them.

I went to take another drag of my cigar, but finding that it was barely lit, I opened the top drawer on my desk to get a lighter. The little BIC was on my paperwork, so I grabbed it. However, something in the back of the drawer caught my attention before I closed it. A photograph I hadn't seen in years was barely visible in the back, but I recognized the silk Gucci button-up I was wearing in it. It had been my favorite shirt over a decade ago. That is until it got soiled with the brains of one of my enemies.

I pulled out the picture and looked at it. I was about fifteen years younger and leaned up against my Ferrari Spider. Standing next to me was my cousin and a man who, at one point, I would trust with my life. Nat Porter. I trusted him so much that I allowed myself to lack behind him. We were family, and we'd known each other since we were kids. So I didn't need to do any background digging on him when he got out of the military . . . or so I thought. He had been good at keeping his business and personal life completely separated. In fact, it wasn't until his funeral that I found out that he had a wife and two daughters—a whole wife and two college-age girls, hidden right under my nose. My jaw clenched. That wasn't the only secret Nat had kept from me.

For years, I traveled the world in search of the rarest relics to add to my collection—all to have some of the most prominent pieces stolen from me—by my own blood. There was no feeling I could compare that betrayal to. I could still remember the feel of the knife in my hand when I shoved it through his heart. All these years later, and I would still make the same decision. Snakes deserved to have their heads cut off.

"Is this a bad time, Zeus?"

I'd gotten lost in a trance staring at that picture. I didn't even notice one of my soldiers standing in the doorway. Trey had been with me for a long time. He'd grown from a boy to a man under my camp. He stood there staring at me with a funny look on his face. It made me wonder how long he'd been standing there. Ironically, he was present years ago when I killed Nat. He had even cleaned up the mess. A bag was hanging from his left hand, so I waved him inside.

"It's never a bad time for my business," I said.

I had Trey doing Kelz's pickups since he was preoccupied with other business. He tossed the bag onto my desk, and I unzipped it. Upon seeing the expected pile of cash inside, I threw one of the stacks at him. He caught it and thumbed the crisp hundred-dollar bills in satisfaction before putting them into his pocket. Instead of leaving right after, he lingered like there was something he needed to say. Finally, he pointed at the picture I'd laid on the desk of Nat and me.

"Do you ever check on his daughters?" he asked.

The question hung over me like a storm cloud. The only time I'd ever seen Nat's daughters was at his funeral. And it was apparent there that they didn't know about me either. I was still so angry at Nat back then that I had never checked up on his family.

"No," I answered.

"You should."

"Should I now?"

"Yeah, you should. You took their—" Trey stopped midsentence when my eyes turned icy. He cleared his throat. "You should just check on them, boss. Family is family."

"Family is family?" I let it soak in for a moment before I chuckled. "I learned a long time ago that family will stab you in the back unless you turn around in time to stab them in the chest. But speaking of families, have you picked up from the Ames family yet?"

"I was on my way to do that when I left here. They've been ducking me all week, it feels like. I don't think they have the money."

"Then you know what to do."

"Fa sho. A'ight, boss. I'm out."

He threw up a peace sign and left my office. I placed the bag of money on the ground and looked at the picture again. There was no use in holding on to pointless memories. I ripped the photo down the middle and tossed both pieces in the garbage. Right when I was about to get back to work, I got another visitor. It was Shalia. The revealing top and leather skirt she wore clung to her body. A big mischievous grin covered her face as she came around my desk and sat on my lap. My hands found their way to her soft bottom, and she planted a wet kiss on my lips.

"I knew I'd find you here. Do you ever leave this office?" she asked.

"The perk of being the boss is that my money works for me. I don't have to leave my home unless I want to. Is there something you need?"

"No, I just came down here to check on my baby. You okay?" She sincerely stroked my face.

"I'm as good as any millionaire can be. Better probably."

"Good, baby. Did you . . . find the journal you were looking for?"

There was much timidness in her voice while asking the question. Almost as if she knew she was crossing over into a territory she wasn't supposed to be in. I cocked my head and surveyed her curiously.

"How do you know about Giovanni's journal?"

"I've just heard you say it here and there. I know it's something you're looking for. I was just wondering if you found it," she told me, shrugging it off.

"I haven't found it yet, but I'm getting close," I said, gently pushing her off me.

I stood up and went to a file cabinet on the other side of the office. I pulled a rolled-up piece of parchment from it and brought it back to my desk. It was something I hadn't shown anybody, but I was so excited about it that when Shalia brought up the journal, I almost couldn't help myself. I unrolled it out on the desk, exposing its contents.

"What's this?" she asked, leaning in to get a better look.

"It's a family tree," I said, pointing at all the names and branches. "But not just any family tree. The Whitlock family tree."

Using my finger, I trailed down to one of the last names on the bottom of the tree and stopped.

"Giovanni Whitlock," she read out loud. "Wait, as in the one the journal is named after?"

"Exactly. Giovanni was very well known and sought after. Somehow, I was able to find his family tree in the confines of a library in New Orleans. Can you believe that?"

"But wait." She leaned closer. "Why does his lineage stop after him?"

"That's exactly what I've been trying to figure out. He had to have children. It's said the journal was passed down from generation to generation, but it looks here like the Whitlock name died with him. And I feel that's impossible."

"Maybe it did die off."

"I just told you that's impossible."

"Not if he changed his name," she said and wagged a finger my way.

"Interesting," I said as her words settled. "Hm. Thank you."

At that moment, Kiara walked into the office and rolled her eyes, seeing Shalia there. The vein popping out of her temple proved that the mere sight of Shalia made her nerves bad. It had taken Kiara time to warm up to all the girls, but it had never taken this long. She just flat-out didn't like the girl. The eye roll was met with a smirk from Shalia as she gave me another kiss on the lips.

"I'll see you later, baby," she said, looking deep into my eyes.

"Okay," I said, and she slowly and seductively walked out of the room.

When she was gone, Kiara shut the door, and I rolled up the family tree to put it away. Kiara moseyed up behind me and tried to get a glimpse of what was in my hand.

"What's that?" she asked.

"Business."

"Business that you can't tell me about?"

"Business I don't want to talk about."

"With me."

"Excuse me?" I asked.

"You meant to say business you don't want to talk about with me," she said, annoyed. Then as I locked up the parchment, she sat on my desk and leaned back on her hands. "Why can you tell *her* about it and not me? She hasn't been here long enough to know anything about your affairs. That bitch is just here for the gifts."

"If I recall, it was the gifts and glam that caught your attention too," I said, walking over to her.

"You reward me with gifts and a great life for my loyalty and devotion to you. That bitch has barely put in any work."

"Why don't you like her?"

"I just don't trust that bitch. I like to listen to my gut."

"You know I depend on you to keep the others in check. So you need to be nicer to her."

"As I said, I don't trust her."

"Hmm," I said and positioned myself between her legs. "Are you sure you aren't jealous of all the time she spends with me?"

"No," she said and looked away. I turned her head back to face me.

"Do you think I fuck her like I fuck you?"

"Do you?" she asked, and I shook my head.

"I enjoy them and appreciate the things they do for me. But you're the only one I love," I told her. "Do you believe me?"

"Sometimes. You used to do things to make me feel special. Now, I feel equal to them."

I leaned so close to her that my lips brushed her ear. I felt her take in a sharp breath when my hands gripped the fabric of her dress to hike it up. I moved her panties to the side and slid a finger up the slit of her moist cat, stopping once I felt her clit. I softly sucked her earlobe while my finger circled the key to her pleasure.

"What can I do to make you believe me all the time, hmm? Will fucking you on this desk help?"

"Maybe," she breathed back.

"Maybe isn't good enough. What if I take you on a trip to Lagos? Just me and you. Will that help?"

"Yessss," she said with a moan.

Her legs opened wider for me, and with my free hand, I undid my pants, releasing my one-eyed monster. My finger had become sticky and drenched from her juices. I stopped teasing her and put my hands behind her knees as I positioned myself to disrupt her insides. Our eyes met as I slid into her tsunami, and I watched her face twist in pleasure. I even had to suck in a quick breath through my teeth. Her walls hugged my shaft tightly as if they were welcoming it home.

"Damn," I said, shaking my head at her. "This is why you're my favorite girl."

I plunged deeper until I hit her cervix. Then I pulled out and did it again. And again. Once I found my stroke, the only sounds in the office were Kiara screaming my name. If it weren't for the soundproof walls, I was sure the entire house would be able to hear her.

Turned on, I pulled her off the desk and bent her over it so I had the most delectable view of her big brown ass. I couldn't help myself. I needed a taste. Spreading her cheeks wide open, I licked her from her pussy to her asshole. She quivered as I devoured her, and it made my dick jump.

"Zeus, I love you so much," she moaned. "Oh, I love you so much."

Suddenly, she squealed, and a rush of her juices squirted all over my chin. Her orgasm caught me by surprise but in a pleasing way. I stood up and went in to finish the job. I reentered her pulsing love canal and drilled her until an electric shock came over me. My toes curled in my shoes, knowing it was too late to stop. My fingers bore into the sides of her hips as an explosion erupted inside her. My orgasm instantly wore out my body, and when I pulled out of her dangerous cat, I stumbled backward into a chair.

She pulled down her dress and then came to zip up my pants. Her lips found my forehead before going to where I'd placed the bag of money Trey had brought me. She hoisted it up and put it on her shoulder.

"I'll go put this in the safe and leave you to your work," she said, heading for the exit. Before she left, though, she turned to face me. "I'll try to be nicer to Shalia. But only for you."

"For now, that's all I'm asking."

Nadi

Shopping always did my heart good, but shopping with my family beat all. Nori, my mom, and I had just stepped back into my mom's house. Our hands were filled with so many bags that we had to leave the shopping center before we got robbed. It was hard to miss all the designer store bags in our hands. I had cashed out on all of us without thinking twice about it. We were all worn out as we set our bags down in the middle of the living room. Nori collapsed onto one of the couches, and I fell on top of her. A fit of giggles escaped both our lips as she fought to get me off her. Once she finally managed to, I curled up beside her and rested my head on her shoulder.

"Mommy, why didn't you just get that other Chanel bag like you wanted?" she asked.

"Because I wanted these shoes I got instead," Mommy said from the love seat, pointing at a Gucci bag. "Ooh, thank you, Nadi. I needed that. I haven't had anything new in my closet in ages."

"No problem, Mommy. I know you disapprove of how I got the money."

"I don't," she said, wagging her finger sternly, but then her face broke into a smile. "But that's behind you now. So what do you plan on doing with yourself these days, girl? Hopefully, go back to school."

I made a face. "No. That's Nori's thing. I already jumped off that porch. I want to stand on a new one. I'm thinking of starting my own business."

"What kind of business?"

"I don't know. Maybe a jewelry business," I said. "I think I'd do good in it."

"I think so too. You both have Daddy's keen eyes for treasure, so go ahead, girl. Speaking of treasure, where is the journal?"

I sat up straight. Nori and I exchanged glances.

"I have them put up for safekeeping," Nori answered.

"Them?" Mommy asked.

"I kind of, sort of, made a copy of it."

"You what!"

"It was just for insurance purposes," I told her. "Plus, I think it's best that Nori and I had our own. That way, we can add our own findings to our own journals. That is when I dive back into it."

"I think that's a smart idea," Mommy said and stood up. "Now, if you'll excuse me, I'm going to try on my shoes with that dress I've never worn."

She left us in the living room alone, and Nori smiled at me before getting more comfortable to scroll through her phone. She'd been in much lighter spirits since I'd been around more. That was why I hadn't had the heart to tell her I'd spoken to Kelz. And I definitely didn't tell her that I'd agreed to work with him again. I didn't want to keep any more secrets from her, but I also didn't want to hear her mouth. I prepared to take a nap until my mom started dinner, but my phone ringing stopped that plan. It was Kelz.

A little over a week passed since I had seen him, and we'd only talked a few times since. But it wasn't like I was just sitting waiting by the phone or anything. Okay, I had been. Kind of. I guess I was expecting him to blow up my phone once he knew he was unblocked. He said he would show and prove, but it was always about business every time we talked. I glanced at Nori and saw that she was giving me a weird look. I excused myself and got up from the couch so that I could go and answer it.

"Hello?" I said into the phone once I was locked away in the bathroom.

"Tonight's the night," his deep voice said.

"You sure you need me? You and Banks handled those first two just fine by yourselves."

"That was something that just happened. But tonight, I do need you. Did you look over what I sent you?"

Days earlier, Kelz told me Nicolo Brasi was opening a new Italian restaurant called Brasi's downtown. The building was an old storage warehouse, but Banks found out that Nicolo had bought it out. He turned it into a fine dining spot. The grand opening was publicized and all over social media. However, entrance was invite-only, which proved difficult to get around until Kelz pulled a play from my book. He found the blueprint of the building when it was a warehouse. It hadn't done me much good, though. I drove past the restaurant a few times. From the outside, I could tell that Brasi had completely changed the place. The blueprint was almost useless.

"I looked at it. But I would need the current blueprint to make anything work inside the restaurant," I told him.

"Well, tonight is the night we know where Brasi will be and when. So we have to make something shake. I'ma call you back. Let me call Banks."

"Wait, I said I can't make a play for the inside of the restaurant. I didn't say I can't make some shit shake," I said while examining my freshly manicured nails. "The grand opening is invite-only at eight o'clock, right?"

"Right."

"Okay, then. Fuck the grand opening."

"What?" Kelz asked, clearly confused.

"Just like I said, fuck the grand opening. I drove by the place earlier today while shopping with my family. They're still working on getting their security system up and running in the back. From the look of it, it might take some time. But that's not the only thing I noticed."

I paused for dramatic effect and laughed softly when I heard Kelz's exasperated sigh on the other end of the phone.

"Are you going to tell me, or do you want me to die from suspense?"

"I saw a ladder. The inside of Brasi's might be off-limits, but I didn't say anything about the roof. Have Charles and Coney head down there early and position themselves on top of the restaurant. Banks can cover one flank, and we'll cover the other. I'm sure Brasi will be covered when he steps out of the car, but when that showy bastard steps on the red carpet, the shot will be clear."

"How do you know he'll stop on the red carpet?"

"As I said, he's a showy motherfucka. Have you seen his Instagram? He's going to want something to post, trust me. Too bad all his followers will be saying RIP by the morning. Let the others know what's up, and come pick me up at the hideout later. P's and Q's, Kelz."

"Okay, boss," he joked. "And, Nadi, tomorrow, let's do dinner. I'll take you to your favorite restaurant, and then we can return to my place for dessert."

I stifled my giggle, but my smile was so big I could feel the air on my teeth.

"Dinner sounds fine, but don't push your luck."

I disconnected the call. I hated that I would miss dinner, especially since Mommy was making her famous fried chicken and cabbage, but duty called. Before I left the bathroom, I checked my reflection in the mirror. I just wanted to get through that night so I could get to tomorrow night. Kelz had some major making up to do, so hopefully, he'll pull out all the stops. I opened the door to step out and almost ran right into my sister. I furrowed my brow and wondered how long she'd been standing there. By the disappointed look on her face, it had been long enough.

"I knew it was him when you couldn't take the call in front of me. I *knew* it was Kelz," she exclaimed, shaking her head.

"Shhh," I said and glanced down the hallway to make sure our mother hadn't heard her. "Why are you all up in my business anyway?"

"Because I thought you were done with him. What is it now? Does he have you stealing some rare necklace now? Or maybe it's another golden sword."

"I said I was done with that, and I meant it," I hissed. "This is something completely different. I have to make money somehow. Zeus needs us—"

"Zeus? You have *got* to be kidding me. Please don't tell me you've gotten yourself caught up with him. You know what Mommy used to say about him."

"He's a no-good drug dealer, I know. But he's also wealthy and powerful. Nori, once I do this, I'm done—both Kelz and me. We're out of the game for good. I promise."

"Yeah, right. Is *that* what he told you?" she scoffed.

I wanted to wipe the smirk off her face, but she had every right to feel the way she did. She didn't have any connection to Kelz to believe in him like I did. I sighed, knowing that there was no getting through to her. We were the opposite sides of the Libra scale, always thinking it was tipping in our favor. I loved her, but I had to do what I had to do. I hugged her and gave her a farewell kiss.

"Listen, just tell Mommy I had to run. But don't say anything else, okay? Especially not about Kelz or Zeus."

She made some noise and went back to the living room. I hoped it meant she would keep her mouth shut.

Chapter 18

Kelz

We're here. Everything is everything.

I read the text from Charles before placing my phone back into my pocket. We had a little over an hour until showtime, and I had just pulled up to get Nadi. It was my fault we were running late. I hadn't been home all day and had to make a little pit stop before grabbing her. I texted her and let her know I was outside. Minutes later, she appeared at the passenger-side door.

"We should already be in pla—" She stopped talking to smile at the dozen roses in the passenger seat.

"Do you like them?" I asked, knowing she would.

"I love them."

She picked them up and got into the car. Seconds after shutting her door, she buried her nose in them, inhaling their delicate aroma. The flowers reminded me a lot of her. Beautiful and elegant, but if handled incorrectly, you would feel the thorns. And I would never handle her incorrectly again. She set them softly to the side and put on her seat belt when I started to drive.

"You ready for this?" I asked.

"I'm ready to get paid. The others in place?"

"Yeah, they're ready."

"Good. After Brasi, we only have one more, right?"

"Yup, Dub Lewis. And then it's over. It's all over."

I figured I would wait until Zeus ran us all the coins before I told him I was retiring from the game. He had big plans for me to be by his side. I doubted he would take too kindly to me turning down his offer, but I was ready to kick back and enjoy life. Go legit, maybe start a family. I might never experience those things if I stayed in the streets. Somebody could blow my noodles back at any moment. All I needed was my life and the woman sitting next to me, and I would be good.

"You serious about quitting?" Nadi asked.

Was she reading my mind? I looked over at her mystically. She had a hopeful look in her eyes.

"You must have known that's what I was thinking about."

"You changing your mind?"

"Nah. Hell nah. After this, I'm good. The money is good, but what use is it if I won't be here to spend it?" I took her hand in mine, using my thumb to caress it. "Plus, with all the making up I have to do for you, I'm going to need a lot of free time."

"You're right about that," she said and paused. Then she began to laugh. "You know something crazy?"

"What?"

"I have only known you a pinch of my life span, but the thought of living without you makes me sick. You should have seen me before. I could barely get out of bed."

"You did about that money, though," I teased.

"Damn straight!" she laughed. "But for real, Kelz, you can't do anymore shit like what you did. I still find myself being so mad at you. You're lucky I love you so much. And love is forgiving."

"I love you too. So from here on out, it's me and you."

"Me and you," she repeated softly and kissed my hand.

My engine revved as I pressed my foot on the gas. I hopped on the interstate to get to Brasi's quickly. The plan was to be in place before Brasi arrived and take him out when the shot was clear. I hoped the task would prove to be as simple as it sounded.

As I drove, my mind wandered to Banks. I didn't like how he had just killed Cat. But his logic was correct. She saw our faces. However, she had done good by us. She didn't deserve a death like that. But the job was the job. Maybe I was going soft. Or maybe I was just tired. I was glad it would all be over for me soon.

We still had over half an hour to spare when we arrived at the restaurant. Still, I would have expected more people there. Surprisingly, the parking lot was empty. In fact, the only cars I saw were in the surrounding establishments. My brow furrowed, and I double-checked the address Banks sent. We were at the right place, plus I recognized Charles's truck parked a little ways away. The red carpet was on the ground in front of the tall double doors, but no one was there to walk it. I parked the car and strained my neck to look inside the dark restaurant.

"This is the place you drove by earlier, right?" I asked.

"Yeah. But it seems so dead. People should be here by now. It doesn't even look like the lights are on."

"My thoughts exactly."

I pulled my phone out and shot Charles a text to see where he was. Minutes passed, so I texted both Banks and Coney the same message. Nobody got back to me. I felt the hairs on the back of my neck stand up. Something wasn't right. I undid my seat belt and prepared to go check it out. When Nadi made to get out of the car, I stopped her.

"You stay here. I'll go check shit out."

"I'm not letting you go in there by yourself. It could be a setup." She looked at me like I was crazy.

"I need you out here looking out. Let me know if you see anything out of place. I'll be fine."

I leaned over and cuffed her cheek before pulling her in for a kiss. It lasted longer than I intended, but damn, I missed the sweet taste of her lips. When we broke away, she had worry in her eyes, but she nodded and let me go alone. Before leaving the car, I pulled my hood over my head and ran across the street to Brasi's. As I passed, I looked through the glass windows of the dimly lit place and saw that the tables weren't even set inside. Maybe Banks had gotten the dates wrong, and the grand opening was another day. I walked around the building to the back and found the ladder Nadi had spoken about. It was already pulled down. I checked my surroundings before climbing up to the roof.

Once there, I wiped my hands on my pants and looked around. I saw nothing but big blocks of wood, metal, and tools lying around. A small shed-looking thing was on the roof, so I walked toward it.

"Charles?" I called. "Coney?"

Nobody answered. The closer I got to the shed, the more my senses told me something was really wrong. I was about to reach for the knob of the shed when I noticed a thin stream of red liquid by my feet. Blood. I followed it and saw it coming from the other side of the shed. Slowly, I crept around to see where the blood was coming from, and the moment I did, my heart sank.

"Damn," I said.

I balled my fists and put them to the sides of my head, exhaling in anguish. I finally found Coney and Charles. Both were lying facedown in a pile of rubble with bullet holes in their heads and backs. They weren't moving, but I still checked their necks to see if I could feel even the faintest pulse. Nothing. I hadn't felt sadness like this in a long time. It ate away at my insides. Charles and Coney had been my friends. They were loyal and followed orders to the end. Grinding my teeth, I fought back the tears that wanted to fall from my eyes.

They'd been facing the side of the street where the restaurant's entrance was. Whoever had killed them must have crept behind them. It hit me suddenly that the killer could still be on the roof. Then behind me, I heard footsteps approaching. Drawing my gun, I whipped around, preparing to shoot whoever it was.

"Whoa, what the fuck, Kelz," Banks shouted, staring at me with huge eyes.

He threw his hands in the air when he saw the gun pointed in his direction. Instantly, I let the gun fall to my side.

"Banks, where the fuck were you?"

"Where I was supposed to be at. Where were *you?*"

"In position. Until I saw wasn't nobody at this motherfucka. And then Charles and Coney weren't answering the phone, so I came to check on them."

"Where they at anyways?" Banks said, swiveling his head to look around. "They were supposed to be here before we even showed up."

"They're right there."

I stepped out of the way so that he could look around the shed at the dead bodies of our friends. When he saw them, a small shout left his lips. He pressed his palms against his face and shook his head.

"Fuck," he shouted. "Fuck."

"Aye, keep it down. Whoever did this could still be here."

"They killed my potnahs," he exclaimed, looking down at their lifeless shells. "This ain't right. I fucked up."

"We need to go. Now."

I hurried back to the ladder, but Banks stopped me.

"Wait, there's something inside that you need to see," Banks said.

"For what, and why were you inside?" I asked.

"When I saw that it was empty, I thought it would be better to get inside and wait there. Just in case y'all missed your mark."

"The front door was open?" I asked with a raised brow.

"No, crazy. I broke in. And then I saw that nobody was here and couldn't possibly be comin', so I started snoopin' around. You won't believe the shit I found. It's big, and your boy, Zeus? He's a snake. Come on."

Before I could say another word, he took off to the other side of the roof, where there was a stairway door. It must have been how he got to the roof. I glanced down toward where my car was parked and felt the urge to go home with Nadi, but I went after Banks instead.

We walked down a stairway that led to the kitchen. Everything was stacked neatly and ready for whenever the place opened up. I stared at the back of Bank's head as I followed him. With each step, I became more and more apprehensive. First, he was wrong about the grand opening, and then he turned around and left his post. In all the time I'd known him, he had never moved like that once. So his doing it twice made me feel like everything wasn't what it seemed.

We reached the front of the seating area, and I stopped walking. Banks continued toward a hallway in the back, but when he realized I was no longer behind him, he stopped too. Turning to face me, the bewildered expression on his face solidified everything for me. Banks *never* showed his true expression on his face. Ever. So the emotion on the roof and him looking at me at that moment? It felt like an act.

"What?" he asked, coming back toward me.

"Banks, what the fuck is really going on?" I asked, still gripping the gun in my hand.

"What do you mean? I'm tryna show you proof about Zeus. This shit was all a setup. He's the reason Charles and Coney are dead. Where do you think I got the information about this grand openin'?"

"Zeus setting us up doesn't make sense." I shook my head. "And even if he did do that, why here? Why now? He had plenty of opportunities to kill me if he wanted me dead. And since when does Zeus talk to you outside of me? I'm the head of this operation, *not* you."

I saw the vein in his right temple pop out. He grinded his teeth and took a deep breath. Then right before my eyes, his whole demeanor changed. It was like watching a demon take over a body. The sadness and confusion left his eyes as he began to leer at me like he had never seen me. No . . . He was looking at me like he hated me.

"You know, ever since we came to this place, you've changed," Banks said.

"*I've* changed?"

"Yeah, motherfucka. You. We used to be best friends. Brothers. But when we arrived here, you adopted that god complex you talk so much about—calling all kinds of crazy shots. Thinkin' I work for you or somethin'. Thinkin' I'm *beneath* you."

"Banks, what are you talking about?"

"You know exactly what I'm talkin' about. And then the unnecessary killin' you've been doin'. It's really started to worry me," Banks said, and I knew then he was crazy. He was talking about himself. "The guard at the manor. The stripper. But I should have known you'd gone off the deep end the night you killed Zaire."

"What?" That was where I drew the line. "Banks, that was—"

"Stupid. *Very* stupid. Because you should have known his brother would come and find you one day."

I saw movement out of the corner of my eye. Out of the shadows of the hallway Banks had been trying to lead me down appeared a man with two masked goons behind him. It was Zayle. There was an icy glimmer in his eyes that I could see even in the bad lighting. He didn't stop walking until he was standing beside Banks. The goons that had come with Zayle stood behind him and Banks as if to protect them. I went to raise my gun, but strong hands grabbed me from behind and snatched it from me. Two of Zayle's men had unknowingly crept behind me to disarm me. I was stuck.

"I never liked you," Zayle started in his gruff voice. "I never saw what Zeus did in you. And now learning that you're the low-life thief that killed my brother . . . You were right under my nose the whole time."

"I didn't kill Zaire," I growled.

"Then why was this in your bedroom?" Zayle said, holding something up in the air. "When you and those two bodies on the roof broke into my home and stole this watch, you should have read the engraving on it. Z. L. D. for Zeus Lamar Daniels. It was a gift from me to him. If I had known that this watch would have led to so much turmoil, I would have never bought it. But then again, it also led me to the killer."

"You're crazy as hell. That shit wasn't in my room. Banks—"

"Banks came forward and told me everything. How you kept it on your dresser as a souvenir for what you did."

"That doesn't even make sense."

"Then why did I find it there when we visited your house today? I was hoping to kill you there and not even have to put on this little show, but things don't always go your way, do they?"

I couldn't wrap my head around how the watch had gotten into my room. I thought long and hard until I remembered the last time Banks was at my house. He'd gone to use the bathroom. That's when he did it. That's when he planted the watch on me. But that meant . . . He was plotting on me, and I didn't have a clue for how long.

"You!" I growled and tried to rush him.

The goon holding me had a tight grip. I couldn't go anywhere. I wanted like hell to kill Banks. The rage inside of me was burning like hot lava. It was his fault Charles and Coney were dead. All I could do was shoot knives at Banks, who laughed in return.

"Guilty. I might have given him your address," Banks said innocently.

"It seems as though Zeus doesn't know much about the man he's trying to replace me with," Zayle spoke again. "He thinks I'm losing my touch, but it's him. Losing my brother opened my eyes to many things around me. The biggest was who is really there when you need them. Zeus wasn't. He didn't even try to help me find my brother's killer because 'business must go on.' But you were in his face the whole time. It makes me wonder if he knew."

"For the last time, I didn't kill him. Do you know anything about the man standing next to you?"

"I can handle Banks. Plus, he's done me a service by making valuable connections and building trust with the Italians."

"What?"

"Ehhh . . . I also might have tipped Brasi off about Zeus's plan to kill him," Banks chuckled. "He wants to work with us to send that same energy back to Zeus. Soon, everything is gonna change 'round here."

"So, which one of you is taking Zeus's place?" I asked.

"You've done us a service by getting rid of Rashad and Lamont. We have a lot more playing field now. So, we'll cross that road when we get to it."

"Actually, I think we should cross it now," Banks said, drawing his gun and pointing it at Zayle's head.

I was surprised by the turn of events. Zayle kept his composure and didn't seem intimidated by the gun in his face. In fact, he gave a husky laugh. However, his expression looked serious, and he looked Banks up and down like he wasn't even worthy to breathe the same air as him.

"What do you think you're doing?" he sneered.

"Takin' out another valuable chess piece," Banks told him. "See, you're a major liability. One, I don't know if you'll run and give Zeus a heads-up. And two, even if you don't give him a heads-up, you'll

most likely try to get rid of me the moment you feel
you don't need me anymore. And, well, can't have
that now, can I?"

"If you think you can take out Zeus alone, you're
out of your mind."

"Little do you know, I already have. I've been in
Zeus's home for months, and he doesn't even know
it. And now that I've earned the Italians' trust,
they'll back me in any way to put Zeus in the dirt. A
new sheriff is in town."

"Enough of this. Kill him," Zayle commanded
his shooters.

I braced myself for the loud sound of gunfire and
to see Banks's body riddled with bullets. However,
nothing happened. In fact, the goons didn't budge
an inch. Furious, Zayle looked at them.

"I said kill him."

Still nothing. It seemed as if they weren't following his orders that night. In fact, it wasn't
until Banks made a motion with his hand that they
did anything. Finally, they removed their masks,
showing that they weren't Zayle's men at all. They
were Italians. A brief wave of panic overcame
Zayle's face as he realized he'd been duped. Banks
grinned devilishly like the Joker seeing his plan
come full circle.

"Your men are somewhere around here. Dead,
of course," Banks told him. "Any last words?"

Zayle said nothing. He just quickly grabbed the gun on his hip, but he barely touched it before Banks's pistol rang out. The bullet lodged between Zayle's eyes, and he fell limp to his knees before face planting. Then Banks casually stepped over him and focused all his attention on me. I kept my eyes on the smoking gun in his hands, trying to think of an escape plan. The death grip the Italian men had on me made it difficult even to wiggle free.

"Now, back to you, Kelz. The almighty fuckin' Kelz. Not so mighty now, are you?" Banks said, waving the gun at me. "You didn't know I had this in me? The ambitions of a boss. The problem is, if you keep your thumb on top of somebody for so long, eventually, they learn how to maneuver under pressure."

"Banks, we're brothers. We can talk about this. You act irrationally instead of using your fucking mouth."

"When I used my mouth, you used your self-proclaimed power to shut me up. I'm done talkin'. It's time for takin'."

That's when I knew I was about to die unarmed and helpless . . . at the hands of someone that I loved. The irony was that Banks would never have to take everything from me because he was someone I would have given the world to. Life was funny that way. As he continued to rant, I glanced out the window, knowing that Nadi was in the car waiting for me. I would break her heart again because I wasn't making it out. There would be no me and her.

"What are you lookin' at?" Banks asked and looked toward the window. When I didn't answer with my words, he searched the pained expression on my face and found it anyway. "Oh, right. Your bitch came with you, didn't she? I can't wait to kill that ho."

"Don't touch her."

"Shut up," Banks shouted and pistol-whipped me across my face, drawing blood. "Like I said, I can't wait to kill her. But first . . . I gotta kill you."

He stepped back and aimed the gun at my chest. He hesitated, maybe thinking I would beg for my life or talk reason into him. I didn't do either. I stood up straight with my shoulders back. My only regret was being unable to right my wrongs in time to make it to heaven. Fury lit Banks's eyes like the fires of hell when he saw that I wasn't scared to die. I knew he wanted my fear. I wouldn't give it to him.

"I'll see you in hell," he said.

"I'll be waiting. Patiently," I said right before he pulled the trigger.

Three shots rang out, and the bullets hit me square in the chest, knocking the wind out of me. The men holding me let me go, and I fell to the ground. Agony. Excruciating agony was the only way to describe the burning sensation in my chest. My breathing was labored, and I felt my life leaving me every second. I looked up at Banks with blurred vision. I could make out his smile.

"I want you to bleed out, but even more, I want you to die alone," he said to me and then turned to the men behind him. "Let's go get that bitch."

Before he left, Banks left me with one last parting gift. With all his might, he stomped my face with his size twelve shoe twice, disfiguring it. The last thing I felt before I was left there was the feel of their spit on my face.

I knew I was alone when I didn't hear anyone around me breathing. Darkness began swarming around me, and I knew it was just death calling my name. I summoned all my strength to my right hand to pull my phone out of my pocket. I wanted to tell Nadi goodbye. I wanted to tell her I loved her. But even with all the strength I had left, it wasn't enough. My hand flopped at my side, and I was snatched into the abyss.

Chapter 19

Nadi

My leg bounced quickly with anticipation as I waited for Kelz to return to the car. I wanted to text him to see what was happening, but I didn't. If his phone wasn't on silent, I didn't want to give his location away just in case something happened. However, five minutes turned into ten, and he still wasn't back. He should have sent me a message telling me things were good by then. Then unexpectedly, I saw movement coming from inside the restaurant. I didn't know what it was, but something told me to find out.

The very moment I opened the car door was the same time I heard a gunshot. I quickly ducked, but then I realized it had come from inside the restaurant. Okay, I really needed to get in there. Whatever was happening wasn't good. I pulled my gun from its holster and checked my surroundings. I didn't see anyone suspicious as I used the night sky to shield myself as I ran to the restaurant front. Ducking, I peered into the window and saw something that stunned me.

"Italians?" I said to myself.

But that wasn't all. It was Banks. He was standing with the dead body of a Black man at his feet. There was a smoking gun still in his hand, and I gasped when I saw who it was pointed at—Kelz. Two big Italians were restraining him as Banks put the gun directly in front of his chest. I stood up to jump into action, but I moved too slowly.

Boom, boom, boom!

I felt that pieces of my soul left me with each bullet that went into Kelz. He jerked violently three times, and I opened my lips to scream in torment. However, before any sound came out, a hand covered my mouth and yanked me away from the window. The last thing I saw was Kelz's body falling to the ground. I was dragged back across the street, although I fought to get free. But whoever had me had a tight grip. I wasn't released until someone threw me into a car. Once the passenger door shut, my captor hopped in the driver seat, and I aimed my pistol at him. He was a young Black man around my age. He wore braids and was dressed in all black like me. I had never seen him before.

"You can kill me, or we can get the hell out of here, Nadi," he said, starting the car.

"I'll put a bullet in your skull if you even try to move this car."

"We don't have time for this shit, Nadi."

"How the fuck do you know my name? I don't know you."

"You don't, but I knew your father, Nat Porter. We used to work security for Zeus back in the day. He was like a mentor to me."

"See, now I know you're lying. My daddy didn't work for no damn Zeus," I barked. "You have five seconds to tell me who you really are."

"I just told you," he said, looking me in the eyes. I saw panic there, but I also saw sincerity. "There's a lot that you and your sister don't know. For example, you didn't know Nat worked for Zeus, and you also didn't know that they were cousins."

"Cousins?"

"I'll explain on the way, but get that fucking gun out of my face," he shouted. We glared at each other until I slowly lowered the gun. "Thank you."

I kept my finger on the trigger just in case I needed to use my gun after all. He sped off from in front of the restaurant, glancing feverishly into the rearview mirror. When we were far enough away, everything started to hit me like a ton of bricks. Banks. The Italians. The restaurant not really being opened. It was an elaborate setup. One I was sure I wasn't supposed to survive. I bit back my tears. There wasn't time to cry. I needed more information. Like, who was the motherfucka driving me right then? Where had he come from, and how had he shown up at that exact moment? I held my gun up to his head again.

"This again? Didn't I just save your life?" he asked in an exasperated tone.

"I don't know. Did you? Who are you?"

"The name's Trey. I'm a Virgo, and I like long walks on the beach. Preferably with a bottle of Hennessy in my hands."

"You think this shit is funny?" I asked, stopping myself from pistol-whipping him.

"Do you see me laughing? I don't know what the fuck that was back there. All I know is that Zeus has been having me closely monitor Zayle."

"Zayle?"

"The other dead motherfucka back there. He's Zeus's right-hand man. Or was. Zeus hadn't trusted him for a long time, but he wanted proof before he knocked off Zayle. I got all the proof tonight that he was trying to work with the Italians. But whoever that killer with mommy issues was back there, he took Zayle off the map before Zeus could. Who is he?"

I took in Trey's words and let them land in my mind. If he had been following the Zayle person, it explained why he had been there that night. I let my gun fall again and leaned into my seat.

"We used to work together for a while."

"Doing what?"

"I don't know you enough to tell you my business. Just know he's a snake. I always felt that about him, but Kelz . . ." I started choking up again. I cleared my throat before I continued. "They were like brothers. And Banks killed him."

"I knew they looked familiar. Zeus wanted Kelz to be bigger than big in these streets. Said he had more than the makings of a king, that he was one already. Damn, he ain't gon' be happy to hear he died. And I ain't gon' be happy because I'm the one who has to go clean up the mess."

"Don't call him that," I snapped. "Kelz has never and will never be a mess."

"My bad," Trey said and glanced over at me. I didn't even try to hide my grief. "He was your man, huh?"

"Yes. And we were going to leave all this shit behind us."

"He must have really loved you to leave it all behind," he said absentmindedly as he drove.

His words echoed throughout my head. He was right. Kelz did love me, and I knew he did. Still, I was trying to make him prove something I already knew. He was going to give up everything for me—for us. Now, he was gone, and I was left to pick up the pieces. It wasn't like the last time. This time, he was dead.

"Can you take me home?" I could barely speak the words.

"You sure it's safe?"

"Banks doesn't know where I live. I'll be fine. I just need to be with my sister." Trey still looked skeptical about taking me home. I didn't understand why he cared so much. "Just take me home."

"Okay, okay. Shit. I'll take you home. Just don't point that gun at me again."

I gave him directions to my place. The nightlife sights of LA were a blow to me. I was numb to everything. I didn't want to think about what happened, but it seemed to be the only thing I could think of. I didn't even realize we'd reached my condominium until the car stopped. I tucked my weapon away again and opened the door. Before I was out, I looked back at Trey.

"Thank you," I told him.

"No doubt. I'll be in touch."

"Why?"

"You might need some protecting," he said like it was nothing. "Plus, I should have reached out a long time ago. You know, after your pops died."

I nodded, and when I shut the door, he pulled off. I didn't even know if Nori was home, but I hoped she was. When I walked in, the doorman spoke to me, but I said nothing back. I couldn't find the energy. Somehow, I made it up the elevator and to my door. Before I could put the key in the lock, the door flung open, and Nori stood there with her hands on her hips. She was wearing a pair of pink silk Prada pajamas and a bonnet on her head. The stern look on her face quickly faded when she saw me in distress.

"Nadi, wha—are you okay, sister?"

"It's Kelz," I started, finally allowing the ocean to build up in my eyes. "He's . . . He's dead. Nori, Kelz is dead."

Saying the words out loud took the last of my energy. I fell into her arms, and she caught me. We both fell to the ground, and she held me tight as I bawled into her shoulder. I didn't know how long I cried, but it seemed forever. My sobs filled the home with deep sadness and sorrow. By the time I was done, I was sure my eyes were puffy and bloodshot.

"Nadi, what happened? Are you hurt?" Nori asked, gently pushing me away slightly by the shoulders.

"No, not physically hurt. It was all a setup. Banks, he killed Kelz."

"What?" Nori's hand went to her chest. "I thought they were like brothers."

"Yeah, me too," I sniffled. "I'm sure he would have killed me too if I hadn't gotten out of there."

"I'm glad you did. Something told me to come home instead of staying at Mommy's. Oh my God. I didn't like Kelz very much, but I am *so* sorry, Nadi. I can't even begin to imagine your pain right now."

"I think—" I paused to wipe the remaining wetness from my face. "I think we should move, Nori, away from California. You graduate soon. I just want to start over somewhere new."

"Okay," she agreed with a nod. "You, Mommy, and me."

We hugged again tightly, and I wished that simple gesture could heal me. But it was only enough to keep the tears from falling again. I didn't want to move yet. Then suddenly, the house phone began ringing in the kitchen. Nobody but our mother knew that number, and she would call it back-to-back if we didn't answer our phones. Nori helped me to my feet, walking me to a recliner before going to answer it.

"Nori, don't tell her about this, okay?" I said, resting my head on my hand.

My eyes closed, and I tried mentally to go somewhere far from there. It didn't work. Nothing would change the fact that the love of my life was gone.

"Hey, Mommy. I'm here with Na—Hello? Who is this?"

I opened my eyes and sat up when I heard the concern in her voice. I mouthed, "Who is it?" She didn't answer me, but I swore I saw her grow pale in seconds as she listened. I thought that maybe Banks had found me and was threatening us. I would kill him.

"Nori, who is it?" I asked, standing up.

"Oh my God. Okay. Okay, we'll be right there." She was in distress, and her hand trembled as she hung up. Finally, she turned to face me with streams of water coming from her eyes. "Nadi. Nadi, it's Mommy."

"What . . . What about Mommy?" I rushed over to her and grabbed her hands. "Nori, what happened to her?"

"There was a terrible accident. She fell down the stairs in her house. She's in the hospital. We have to go now!"

Chapter 20

Zeus

The hospital was bright and busy that afternoon. I walked to the front desk with a bouquet and tapped the glass. The young woman sitting behind the desk looked up, and I smiled charmingly. She seemed to melt the moment my white teeth flashed. The corners of her rosy lips lifted as she sat up straight.

"H-how may I help you, sir?"

"Chasity Porter's room, please."

"Just a second," she said, typing a few things into her computer. "There she is. She's up on the third floor in room 317."

"Thank you," I said with a wink.

"Your wife?"

"Family friend," I answered and walked to the elevators.

Chasity Porter, wife of my late cousin. Information about her nasty fall had briefly made the news that morning, and I wanted to visit her. Her friend found her late in the evening last night. She was barely conscious and would have died had her friend not called for an ambulance. The entire community was asked to pray for her speedy recovery.

I took the elevator to the third floor and went to room 317. The closer I got, the louder I heard cries coming from within. Finally, I stopped in the doorway and observed the scene. Chasity lay asleep in a hospital bed, hooked up to a few machines. On either side of the bed sat two young women who looked identical to Nat Porter. I'd only seen his daughters once before, but I recognized them. One was crying softly, and the other held her mother's hand. I would have been moved had it not been for the events that had occurred the night before.

Seven o'clock the previous night . . .

Knock, knock.

My large knuckles rapped against a tall, brown door. I stepped back and waited patiently for it to be answered. I knew someone was inside the two-story home because I saw the lights on and the shadow of someone moving around through the window.

"Just a second, girl!" a pleasant voice called. Moments later, the door swung open. "My bad, girl. I was putting on my—It's you."

The pleasantries in her voice faded as quickly as they sounded when Chasity saw me standing there. It looked like she was getting ready to head out for a night on the town. Her little black dress accentuated her figure, and her updo brought out all the lovely features on her face. From her doe eyes to her full lips, I could see why Nat kept her a secret from a man like me, especially back then. I didn't want one woman. I wanted all of them. I returned her disdainful look with a cheery smile and pointed inside the house.

"I'm going to come in," I said and stepped inside, lightly pushing her out of my way. I looked around at the tasteful decorations of the home. "What a beautiful house. I love the red accent wall in the living room. It brings out the gray furniture nicely."

"What are you doing here, Zeus?" she asked, looking out the door as if someone else were there.

"It's just me. Relax. Shut the door," I said. She tensely shut the door. "This is a matter I wanted to address alone."

"If it's not to tell me exactly how my husband ended up with a stab wound to the chest, I'm not interested," she said, pushing past me to get a pair of heels by the steps.

"Unfortunately, no. I'm sorry, but the killer was never caught." I faked a sincere tone. "His death was hard on all of us."

"Yeah, right. I wouldn't be surprised if you had something to do with it. I told him I didn't want him working for a man like you."

"I'm a businessman, Mrs. Porter."

"No, you're a criminal. There's a difference." Once she put on her heels, she grabbed a red purse from a small nearby table. "What is it that you want?"

"A book," I said simply, watching the color drain from her face.

"A book?" she asked and swallowed her spit. She quickly regained her composure and moved a strand of hair from in front of her eye. "What book might that be?"

"A journal."

"The only journals here are the ones my daughters wrote in when they were 5. Sorry."

She tried to return to the door, but my hand on her stomach stopped her. I could feel the tiny trembles her body was emitting. She had a superb poker face, but the truth of the matter was she was afraid.

"I'm talking about Giovanni's journal."

"I've never heard of such a thing. Now, if you please, leave."

"Hmm," I said, dropping my hand from her stomach. I went to close the curtain on the front door and locked it. When I turned back around, Chasity backed away to the staircase. "You know,

I've been searching for that journal for a very long time. I looked high and low multiple times and came up with nothing. After all these years, I finally found a family tree. The Whitlock family tree. I thought I stumbled across a gold mine, but in the end, it just led me to another dead end. The Whitlock name ended with Giovanni."

"What . . . What does that have to do with me?" she asked softly.

"I didn't know myself in the beginning." I wagged a finger at her. "At first, I thought the name couldn't end with him because the whole tale of the journal surrounds the fact that he passed it down. But to whom if his line died with the name Whitlock? It wasn't until a little birdie gave me a thought. The Whitlock's name died because he changed it. It's so profound yet simple.

"I did some digging. It appears as though Giovanni might have changed his name, but his love for the work he did stayed the same. He'd gone underground, but a few documents from a tomb found in Egypt decades ago mention a Giovanni Pettis. There's another from France that mentions the same name. And another from Italy."

"That doesn't mean anything," Chasity exclaimed.

"It wouldn't if it weren't that both Giovanni Whitlock and Giovanni Pettis allowed themselves

to be photographed. Do you see where I'm going with this, my beautiful Chasity? Giovanni Whitlock and Giovanni Pettis are the same person. So, Chasity, be a dear and tell me your maiden name."

"Go straight to hell."

"You don't have to tell me. The Pettis family tree started with Giovanni and led me straight to you and a deceased cousin named Rebecca. But I knew you were the right choice. It all makes sense now. Why Nat did what he did. He knew I was getting close to finding what I wanted. It was right under my nose the whole time. So where is it, Chasity?"

"I don't have it."

Her lips trembled as she backed up the stairs. I followed her steps, getting in her face. She moved faster, but not fast enough. I was growing tired of her games.

"It was passed down to you."

"I don't have it," she repeated defiantly. "And I'll die before I tell you where it is. I'll die ten times."

We reached the top of the stairs, and I grabbed her wrist before she could run away. She glared up at me as her chest heaved up and down. She was terrified, but the hatred in her eyes told me she meant what she said. She would never tell me where the journal was. To me, that meant one of two things. She didn't know where it was, or she was protecting the person who had it.

"You passed it down already, didn't you? To your daughters."

My words made her doe eyes open wide. I was right. She'd given it to one of them, if not both. She tried to free her arm, but it was no use. I wasn't letting her go.

"Where are they?"

"Stay away from my girls! You stay away!"

"No. And if you don't tell me where they are, I'll have to bring them somewhere I know they'll show up. Say, your funeral?"

"N—"

Before she could scream, I threw her with all my might down the stairs. There was a sickening crunching sound when her head met the marble floor below. Then calmly, I fixed the jacket of my suit and walked down the stairs to leave, careful not to step on her blood . . .

I was going for a funeral, but a hospital room would do. Then I cleared my throat to announce my presence to the girls. Both of them tearfully looked up at me. From the looks on their faces, I was the last person they expected to see.

"I brought these for your mother. I heard about the accident on the news," I said in a concerned voice. "Can I come in?"

"No!" the brown-skinned one said, glaring at me.

"Nadi!" the other said, shooting her sister a look before turning back to me. "That was very nice of you, Zeus. I'll put them on the windowsill with her other flowers."

I looked, and sure enough, the entire windowsill was covered in flowers from family and friends. The one named Nadi hadn't stopped glaring at me since I stepped inside the room. She must have gotten that from her mother.

"What are you doing here? You need to leave."

"Nadi."

"No, Nori. It's *his* fault my boyfriend is dead!"

"And who's your boyfriend?" I asked just to humor her.

I was the reason many women's boyfriends were dead. Unfortunately, it came with the territory. Eat or be eaten alive.

"His name is Kelz. He was doing a stupid job for you, and it got him killed!"

Now *that* was news to me if we were talking about the same Kelz. I furrowed my brow at her, not wanting to believe what she had just said. I had so many plans for him. I was hoping we weren't talking about the same person.

"And somebody named Zayle is dead too. Banks killed them," Nadi continued.

"Banks? Kelz's right-hand man, Banks?"

"Yes."

"Oh, I knew I couldn't trust that slimy mother-fucka," I said to myself, suddenly forgetting why I was there in the first place. "How could he pull off something like that?"

"I don't know. But it has something to do with the Italians. They were there, and it looked like they were working with Banks."

"Wait . . . You were there?"

"I was a part of the team."

The biggest lightbulb lit up my head, and I stared at her like she was a unicorn. She was the key to it all. She was how Kelz found the artifacts. He was sleeping with the keeper of the journal. Just like the chessboard, the queen was always the most valuable piece. I closed my mouth before my jaw hit the floor and gathered myself.

"Banks won't get away with this, I promise."

"Whatever. He already has," Nadi said sadly, looking into my eyes. "Is it true?"

"Is what true, my dear girl?"

"Are you my father's cousin? Our cousin?"

"What?" Nori looked from Nadi to me in a be-wildered fashion.

Apparently, that was news to her as well. I sighed and gave the most pitiful look I could muster.

"Yes, it's true. For a good reason, your father kept his family a secret from my organization. The life he lived working for me was a dangerous one. He didn't want any of you caught up in it. So

I didn't know you girls or your mom even existed until his funeral. And I stayed away because I felt he would want that."

"Then why are you here now? After all this time," Nori asked.

"To right a wrong. To let you know that if anything happens to your mother, I'm here. And you," I looked at Nadi. "If you do the kind of work I suspect, there will always be a place for you in my camp. I need someone I can trust around me."

"I'll pass," she said coldly, and I nodded in respect.

"Well, if you change your mind, this is my address. Come see me any time."

I found a piece of paper and a pen lying around the room and wrote my address on it. I had plans of going about things the opposite way. I planned on finding the journal and then disposing of Nat's daughters, but after meeting them, I was intrigued, especially by how Nadi had flown under my radar for so long. I handed her the piece of paper and left the room. There was no doubt in my mind that she would use it.

When it all falls down, build it up again.

Chapter 21

Zeus

After leaving the hospital, I had some business to attend to. I didn't get home until seven o'clock in the evening. Pamela and Robin were out shopping, and Kiara would be home anytime. I smelled a delicious aroma the moment I stepped foot in the foyer of my house. Standing there to greet me was Shalia wearing a beautiful velvet green gown. Her hair had big curls, and she had done her makeup like she was going to some gorgeous event. She smiled big when she saw me and rushed to hug me.

"Baby, I hope you don't mind. I sent everyone home for the night. I want you all to myself before the others get home."

She kissed me on the lips, and I returned it tenderly. I turned my nose up to the ceiling and took a deep breath. A small moan escaped my lips at the smell of the food.

"Surf and turf." She grinned. "Your favorite."

"You made that?" I asked, surprised.

"No," she admitted and took my hand in hers. "The cooks did right before they left. That Madeline doesn't play about you. She even put your food on a special plate."

"The green one?" I asked, smiling.

"Yes, that one. What's so special about it?"

"It was a part of my mother's favorite fine china set."

She led me to one of the dining rooms in my mansion. That one faced the back of the house where the pool was. The floor-to-ceiling windows encompassed it, and she had set it up nicely with rose petals and lit candles everywhere.

"Do you like it?" she asked, biting her bottom lip.

"I love it," I said.

She pulled my chair out so that I could sit down. She kissed my forehead again and went to the kitchen to grab our plates—the green one for me and a regular white porcelain one for her. The food looked delicious. My steak was cooked just the way I liked it. I waited for her to sit down. However, instead of sitting down at the table with me, she placed her hand on my shoulder. Kneeling, she put her lips close to my ear and whispered.

"This was fun and all, but it's time I go home. Enjoy your dinner." She reached down and pulled my gun from its holster. "Oh, and I'll take this."

Suddenly, a tall figure in a black suit entered the dining room from behind me. He walked to the other end of the rectangular table and sat in front of the plate of food. It was Banks. He looked so pleased with himself. He had won.

"Thank you, baby. You can head home. I'll be there shortly after I finish up here," he said, blowing a kiss at Shalia.

"Okay, baby."

I heard her heels *click clack* as she walked away. When the sound faded, I clapped my hands in Banks's direction.

"Smart man. Using my love of women against me," I said, giving him his props.

"You didn't really think it was a coincidence that you ran into Shalia outside the airport, did you? That was the same day Kelz and I met you for a drop. We knew where you'd be coming from. I sent her there to meet you first."

"Once again, very smart."

"What can I say? You people always doubt the underdog," he said and grabbed a napkin from the table. He tucked it in his shirt and began eating the lobster before him.

I did the same—no point in wasting what was supposed to be my last meal. The savory taste of the steak exploded on my tongue. Madeline got it right every time.

"I assume you're here to discuss business," I said, setting my silverware down.

"Talk?" Banks scoffed as he scarfed down the food. "I'm not here to talk. I'm here to *tell* you what it's gon' be from now on."

"So you're not going to kill me?"

"Oh, I'm most definitely gon' kill you," Banks said. "But before I do that, I want to see the look on your face when I tell you the changes I'm makin' to your organization. First and foremost, anyone with your blood runnin' through their veins will die. Second, I'm liquidatin' all your assets, which you're gon' sign over to me. I mean, a king should be sittin' on gold, right? Oh! And all those treasures we found for you? I'm sellin' them. I don't need that shit. The streets of LA are mine. I even already have a new connect in mind."

"What makes you think you can pull off all of this?"

"Oh, you must not have heard. Nicolo Brasi and I are tight now. And he's ready for war now that he knows you tried to kill him," Banks said between bites. "I told him I would handle it before it got to that point. So it's gon' be just me and him on top."

"You still have Dub to worry about."

"You ain't heard about Dub? Damn, mother-fucka, where have you been? He got his face ate off by some dogs. He's dead. Word on the street is some Crips were behind it. So that leaves all of this for the takin'. Zayle is dead, and Kelz is dead. You have nobody."

His evil laughter pierced my ears. I stared at my plate of food in defeat. He was right. He had severely thrown a wrench into my plans for the future with Kelz. I couldn't believe a snake like Banks was able to take him out.

"Damnit," I said to myself.

"There it is. The almighty Zeus feelin' his defeat. I love this shit," he exclaimed, digging into his steak with gusto.

"I guess this is the part where you kill me. Make it quick. You can at least give me that." I clenched my eyes and fists shut as I lowered my head. Instead of going for his gun, I heard the loud clanking sound of his silverware hitting the plate. "And end scene."

I opened my eyes and grinned across the table at Banks. His hands were still in their positions when they held the silverware. However, he was paralyzed in place. I clasped my hands together and watched him move the only thing he could . . . his eyes.

"Do you know one of the perks of being the most powerful man in LA? I can get information at the drop of a dime. So when I found out you killed Kelz, I did some digging. A rule of thumb . . . Never put your name on a lease. Get a fake ID or something. But the shocker was me seeing Shalia's name beside yours. Ahh, you almost got me." I wagged my finger at him in humor. "Imagine my shock when I found out Shalia was planning a dinner for me tonight. I knew it was a hoax, so I had my cook drug that plate with succinylcholine. The effects aren't long, but they're long enough for this. Kiara!"

Moments later, she came bounding in like the Black goddess she was carrying a big box. She winked at me as she passed and set the box in front of Banks. Then knowing he couldn't move, she pulled the top off for him. When he looked inside, his eyes widened with anguish.

"*Mmmmh,*" he tried to scream. "*Mmmmh . . .*"

Kiara gave a hearty laugh. She had been right about Shalia all along. So it was only fair that I let her do the honors. The box in front of Banks contained two heads—the freshly sawed-off head of Shalia and the slightly aged sawed-off head of Nicolo Brasi. Banks was playing on his own chessboard while I was playing on mine. And on mine, I always win. The sound of the doorbell ringing cut into my plans of torturing Banks, but that was fine. He didn't need to breathe for any extra seconds. I motioned a hand, giving Kiara the green light to rid the world of his stench.

"Finally," she said and pulled out her gun.

"Wait. Quietly. We have guests," I said, raising my brow at her.

She nodded and set the gun on the table, pulling out a knife instead. I got up from the table and went to see who was at the door. As I walked away, I heard Kiara's blade repeatedly piercing Banks's flesh. When I got to the foyer, I fixed my suit before opening the door. The delighted feeling that came to my chest was unexplainable when I saw Nori standing on my doorstep with Nadi.

"Nori, Nadi, what a surprise."

I stepped out of the way and ushered them into the house. I opened my mouth to speak again, but Nadi held up her hand to stop me.

"Look, I'm going to cut straight to the chase. We're used to a certain kind of living, and, unfortunately, you're the only stream that leads us to it," she started. "Nori doesn't get her hands dirty, so perhaps you have something lucrative for her that doesn't involve guns. And me? I'm ready for whatever."

The smile that crept to my face was slow and satisfying. The way things had turned out was even sweeter than I had ever imagined. If Nadi needed to feel like she was running the show, fine. Trust needed to be built, so I would allow it, no matter the cost.

"You don't know how happy I am to hear that. Tell me, have you ever heard of an organization called The Last Kings?"

To Be Continued . . .

The Last Kings Universe in order:

The Last Kings
The Last Kings 2
Deep
Hood Tales
The Nightmare on Trap Street

Five Families of

New York Universe in order:

Brooklyn
Harlem
Bronx
Queens
Manhattan (coming March 2024)